BABYMOUSE
CUPCAKE TYCOON

BY JENNIFER L. HOLM & MATTHEW HOLM

RANDOM HOUSE NEW YORK

AS THE NARRATOR, I REALLY FEEL THAT I SHOULD GET AT LEAST ONE LINE OF CREDIT.

This is a work of fiction. Names, characters, places, and incidents either are the product of the authors' imagination or are used fictitiously. Any resemblance to actual persons, living or dead, events, or locales is entirely coincidental.

Copyright © 2010 by Jennifer Holm and Matthew Holm

All rights reserved.
Published in the United States by Random House Children's Books,
a division of Random House LLC, a Penguin Random House Company, New York.

Random House and the colophon are registered trademarks of Random House LLC.

Visit us on the Web!
randomhouse.com/kids
Babymouse.com

Educators and librarians, for a variety of teaching tools, visit us at
RHTeachersLibrarians.com

Library of Congress Cataloging-in-Publication Data
Holm, Jennifer L.
Babymouse : cupcake tycoon / by Jennifer L. Holm and Matthew Holm. — 1st ed.
    p.   cm.
Summary: When her school library holds a fundraiser, the imaginative Babymouse
is determined to sell the most cupcakes and win the grand prize.
ISBN 978-0-375-86573-2 (trade) — ISBN 978-0-375-96573-9 (lib. bdg.)
I. Graphic novels. [I. Graphic novels. 2. Imagination—Fiction. 3. Contests—Fiction.
4. Libraries—Fiction. 5. Schools—Fiction. 6. Mice—Fiction.]
I. Holm, Matthew. II. Title. III. Title: Cupcake tycoon.
PZ7.7.H65Baf 2009   741.5'973—dc22   2009047346

MANUFACTURED IN MALAYSIA   20 19 18 17 16 15 14 13 12 11 10 9 8

Random House Children's Books supports the First Amendment
and celebrates the right to read.

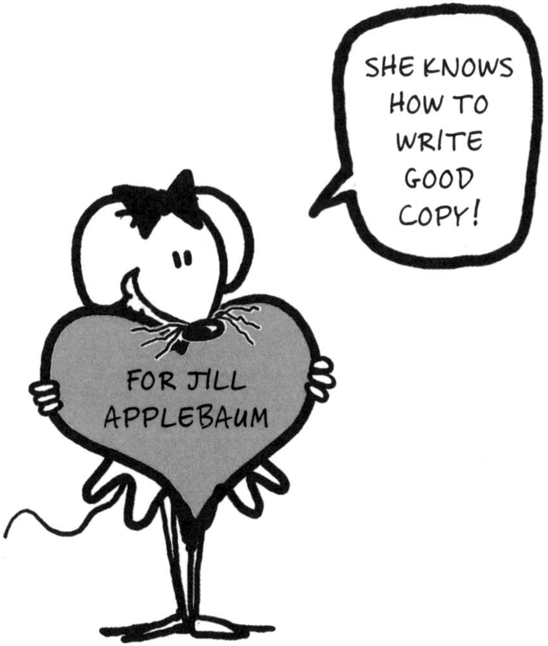
SHE KNOWS HOW TO WRITE GOOD COPY!
FOR JILL APPLEBAUM

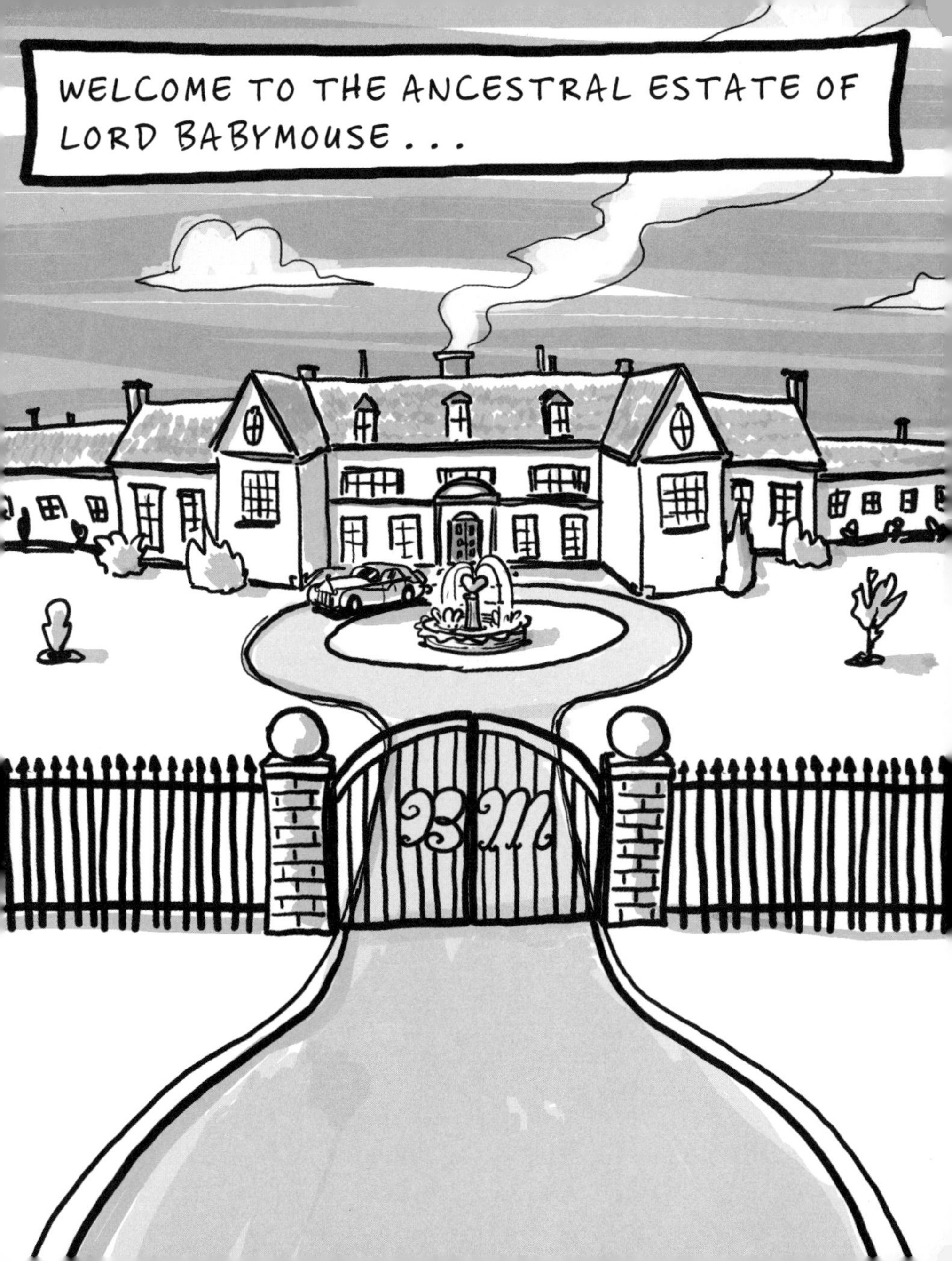
WELCOME TO THE ANCESTRAL ESTATE OF LORD BABYMOUSE . . .

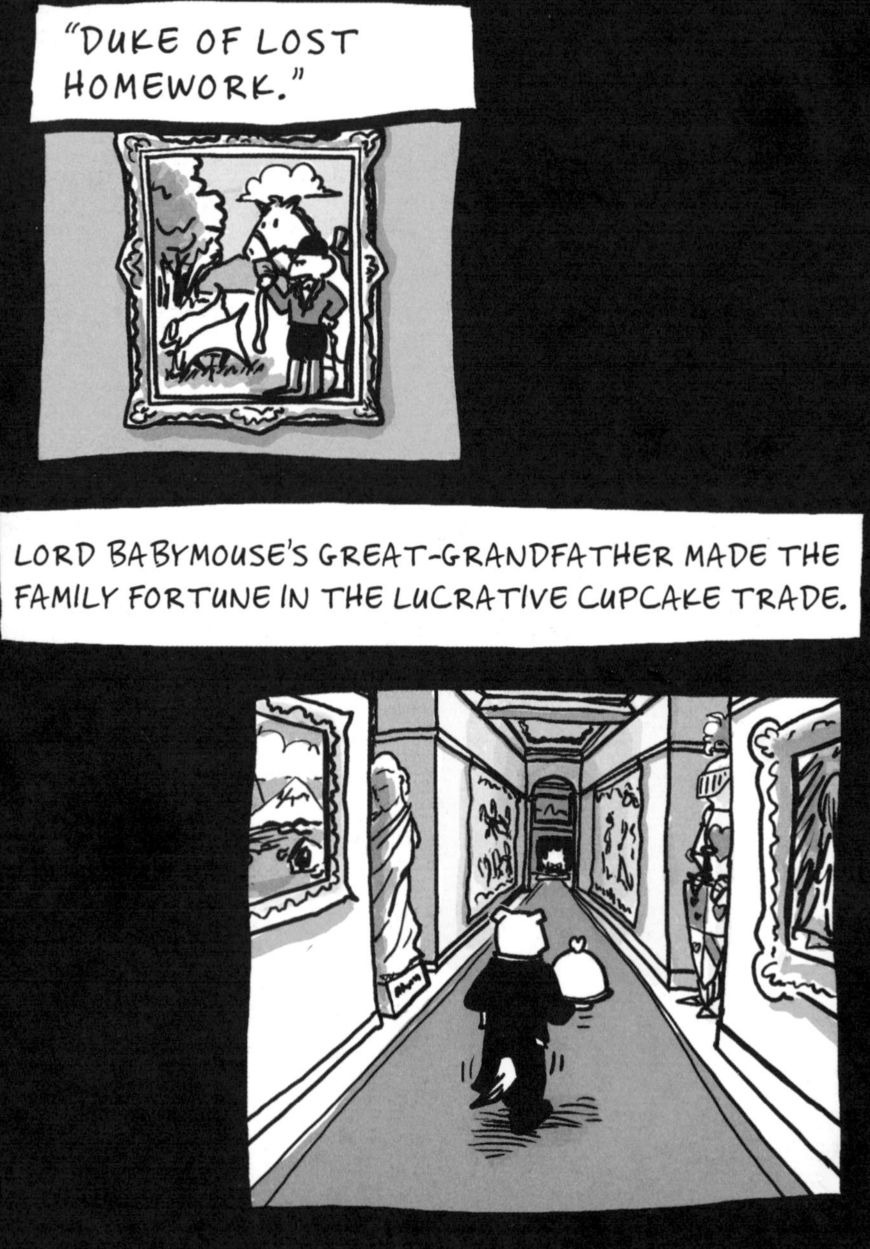
"DUKE OF LOST HOMEWORK."
LORD BABYMOUSE'S GREAT-GRANDFATHER MADE THE FAMILY FORTUNE IN THE LUCRATIVE CUPCAKE TRADE.

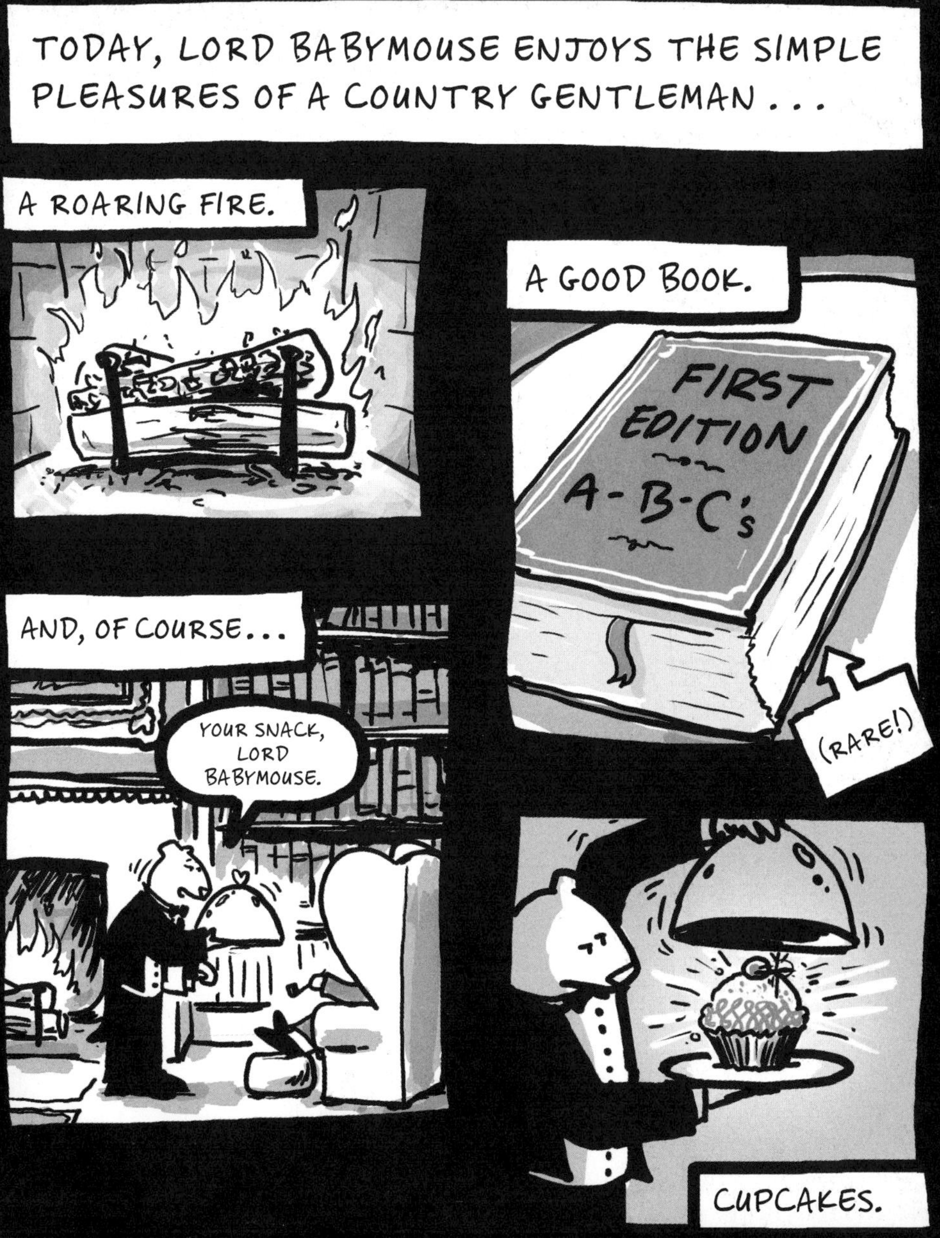
TODAY, LORD BABYMOUSE ENJOYS THE SIMPLE PLEASURES OF A COUNTRY GENTLEMAN . . .
A ROARING FIRE.
A GOOD BOOK.
FIRST EDITION
A-B-C's
(RARE!)
AND, OF COURSE...
YOUR SNACK, LORD BABYMOUSE.
CUPCAKES.

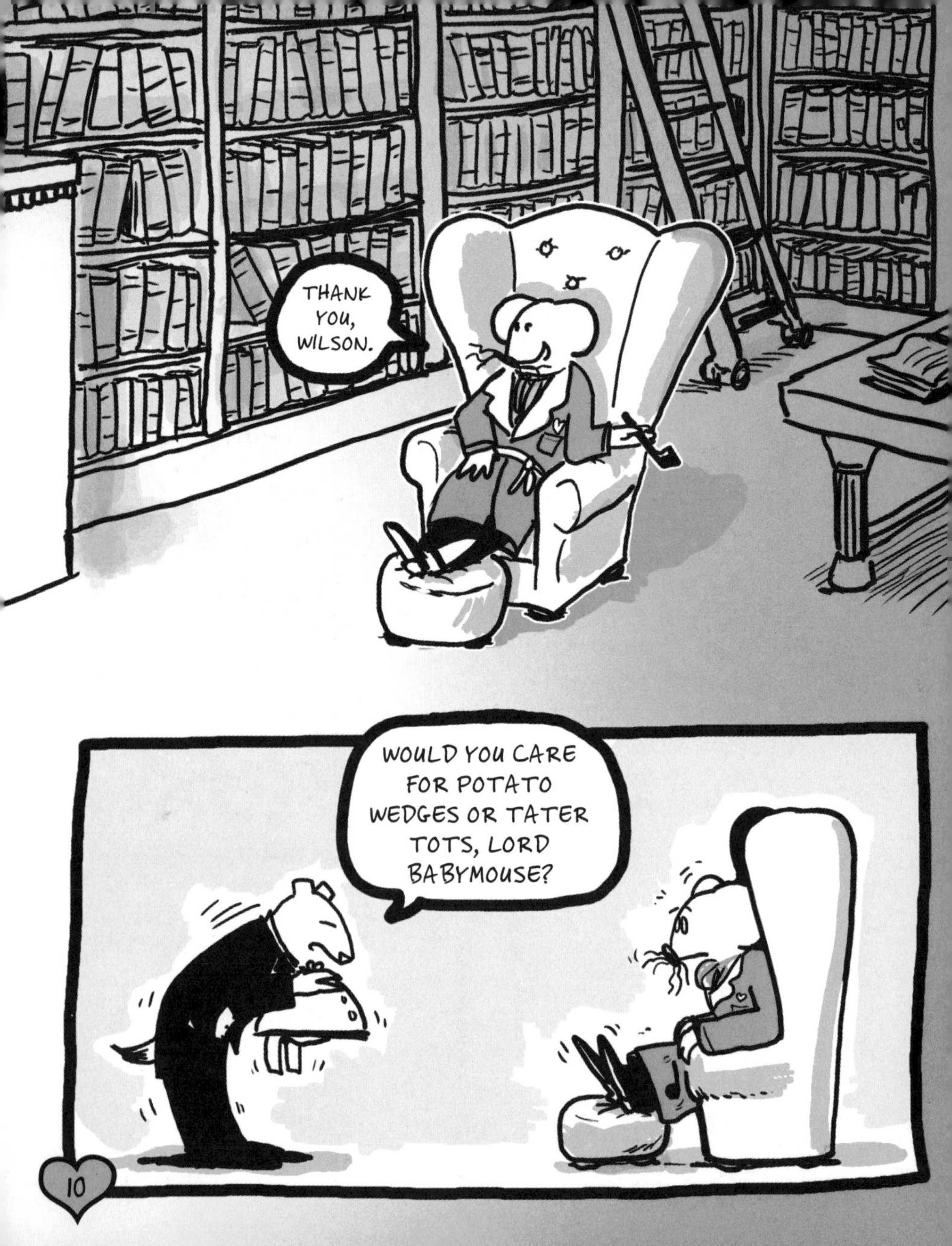
THANK YOU, WILSON.
WOULD YOU CARE FOR POTATO WEDGES OR TATER TOTS, LORD BABYMOUSE?

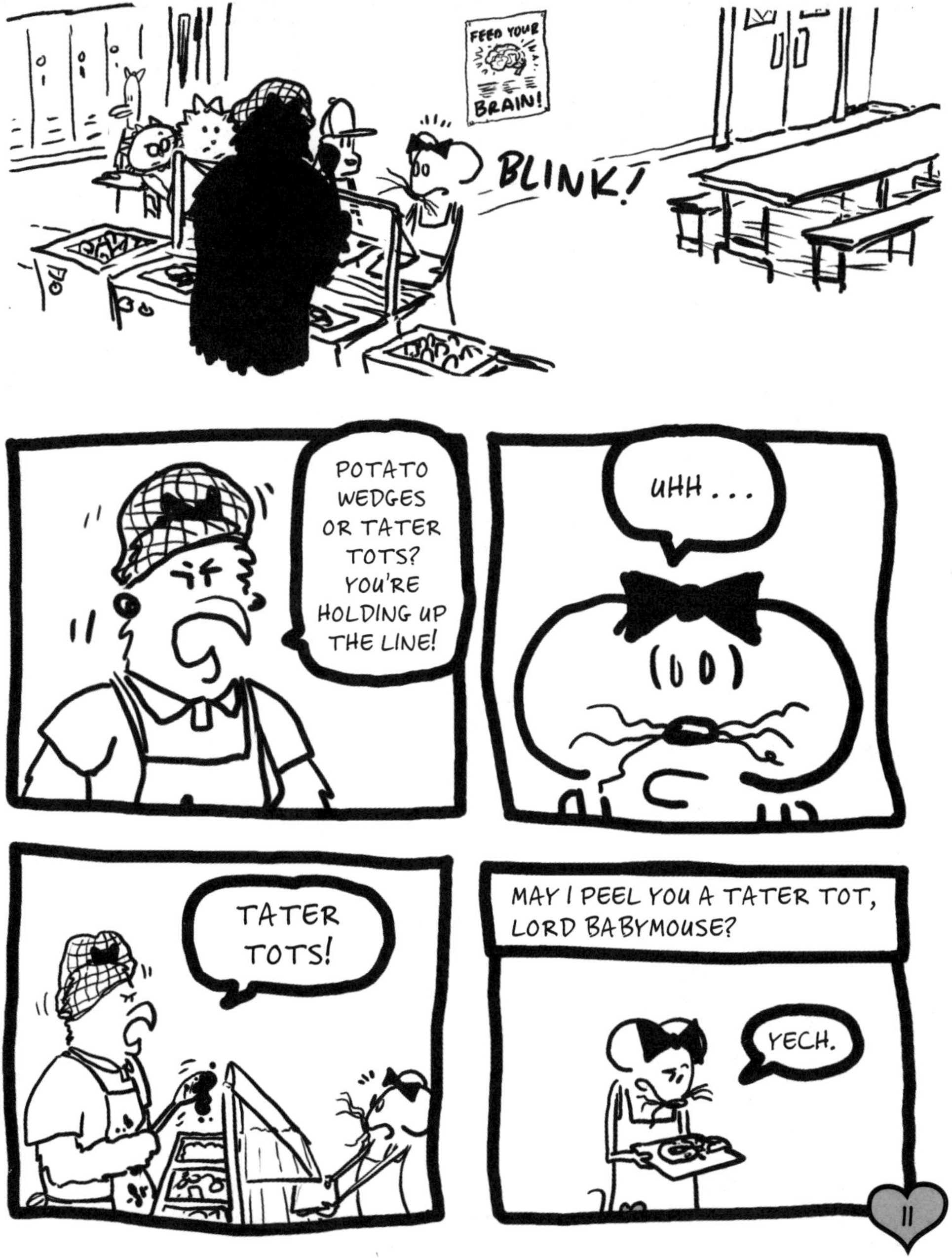
FEED YOUR
BRAIN!
BLINK!
POTATO WEDGES OR TATER TOTS? YOU'RE HOLDING UP THE LINE!
UHH . . .
TATER TOTS!
MAY I PEEL YOU A TATER TOT, LORD BABYMOUSE?
YECH.

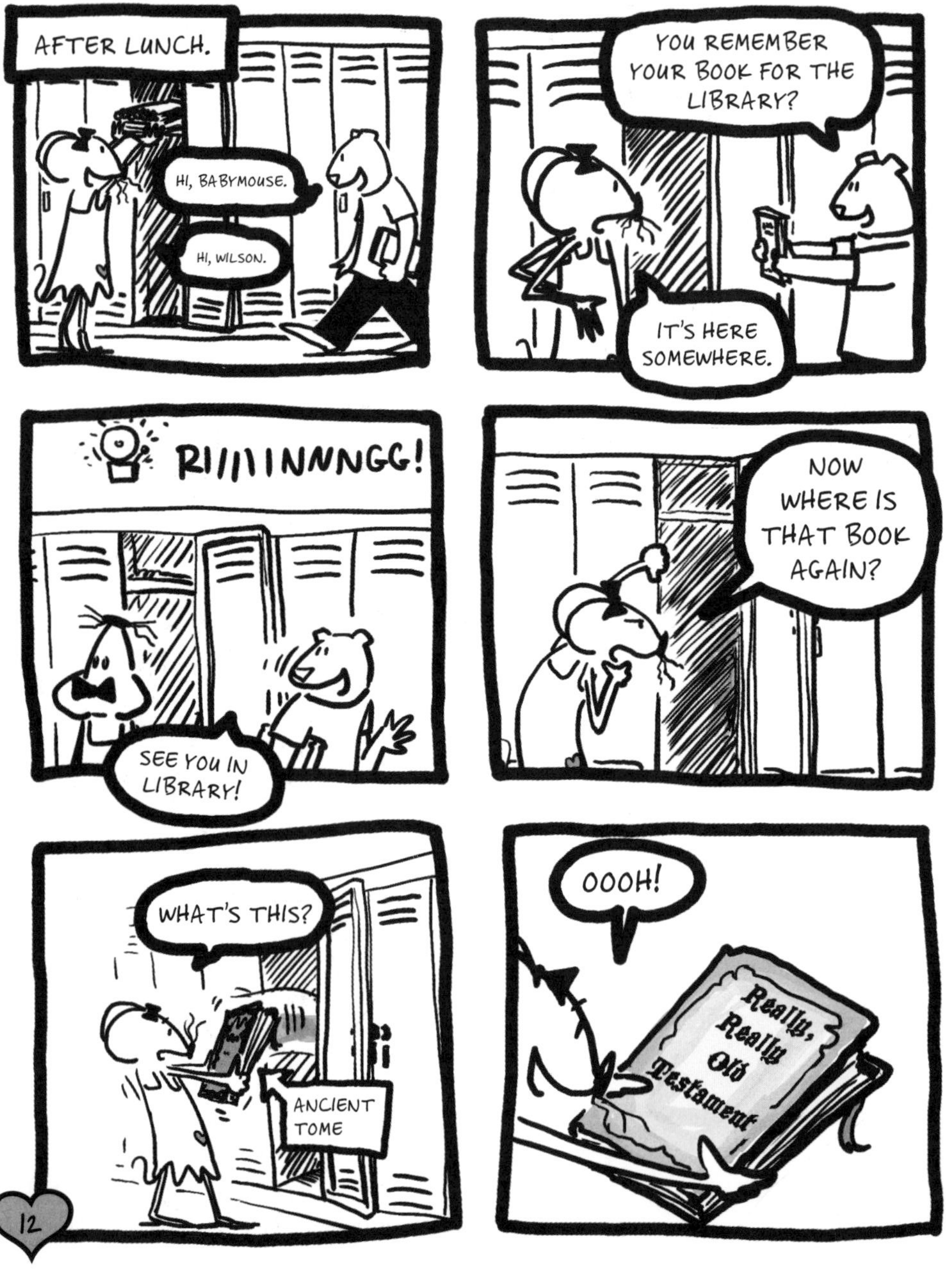
AFTER LUNCH.
HI, BABYMOUSE.
HI, WILSON.
YOU REMEMBER YOUR BOOK FOR THE LIBRARY?
IT'S HERE SOMEWHERE.
RI///INNNGG!
SEE YOU IN LIBRARY!
NOW WHERE IS THAT BOOK AGAIN?
WHAT'S THIS?
ANCIENT TOME
OOOH!
Really, Really Old Testament

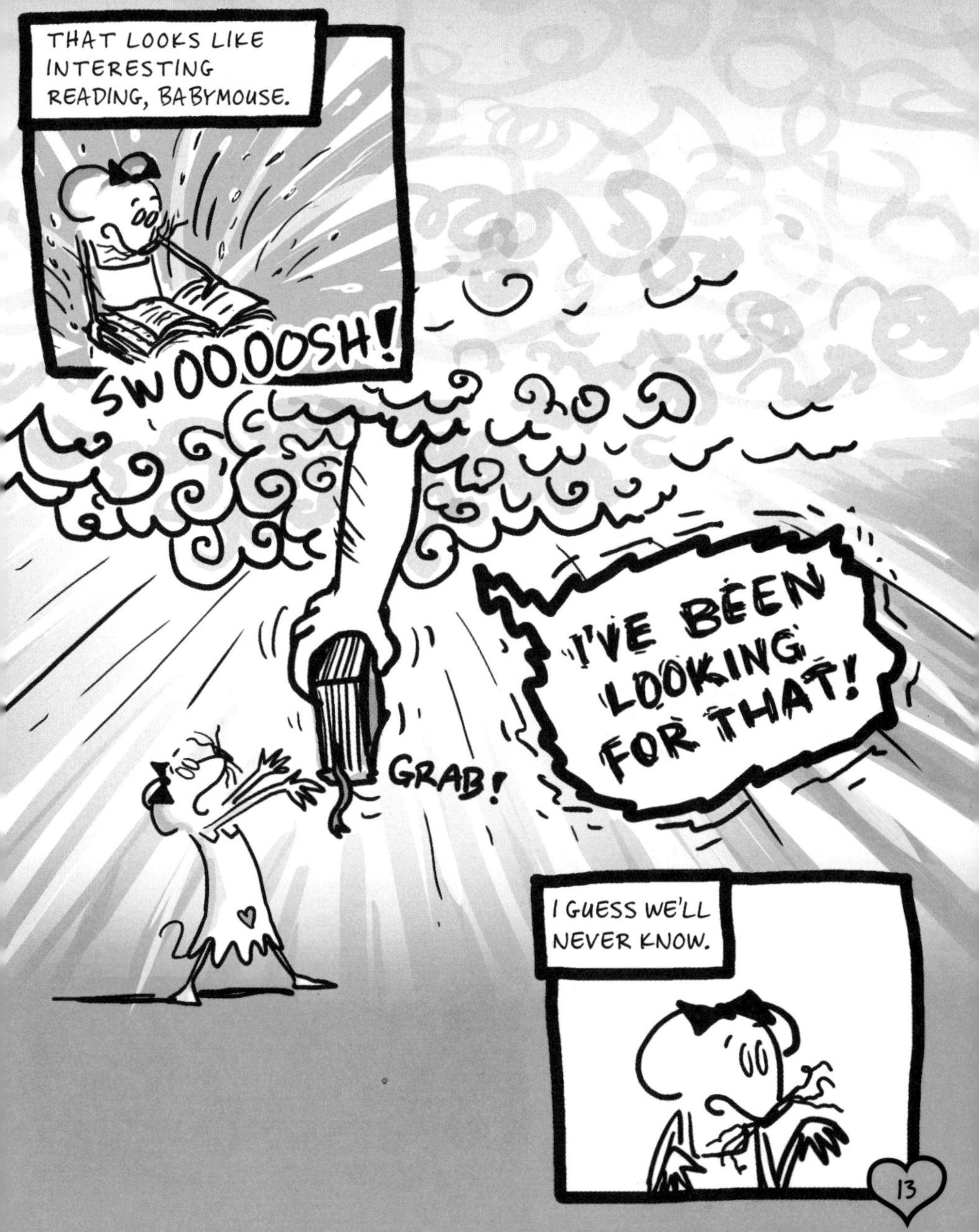
THAT LOOKS LIKE INTERESTING READING, BABYMOUSE.
SWOOOOOSH!
I'VE BEEN LOOKING FOR THAT!
GRAB!
I GUESS WE'LL NEVER KNOW.

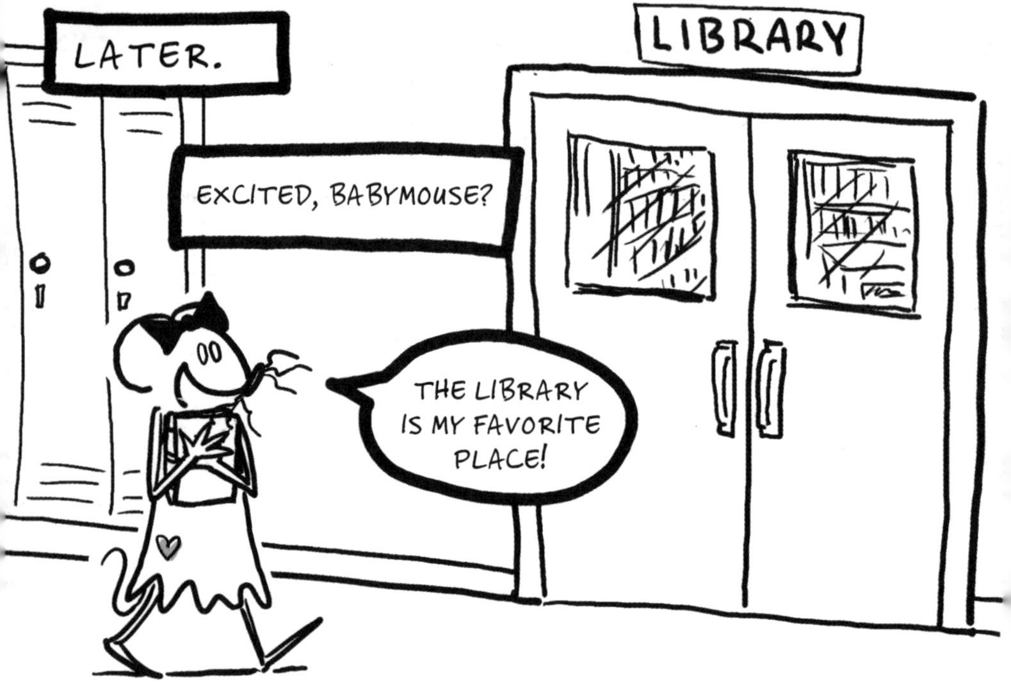
LATER.
LIBRARY
EXCITED, BABYMOUSE?
THE LIBRARY IS MY FAVORITE PLACE!

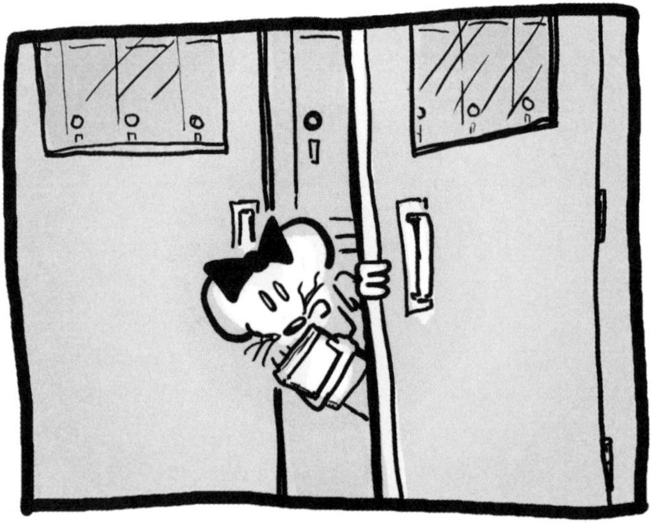

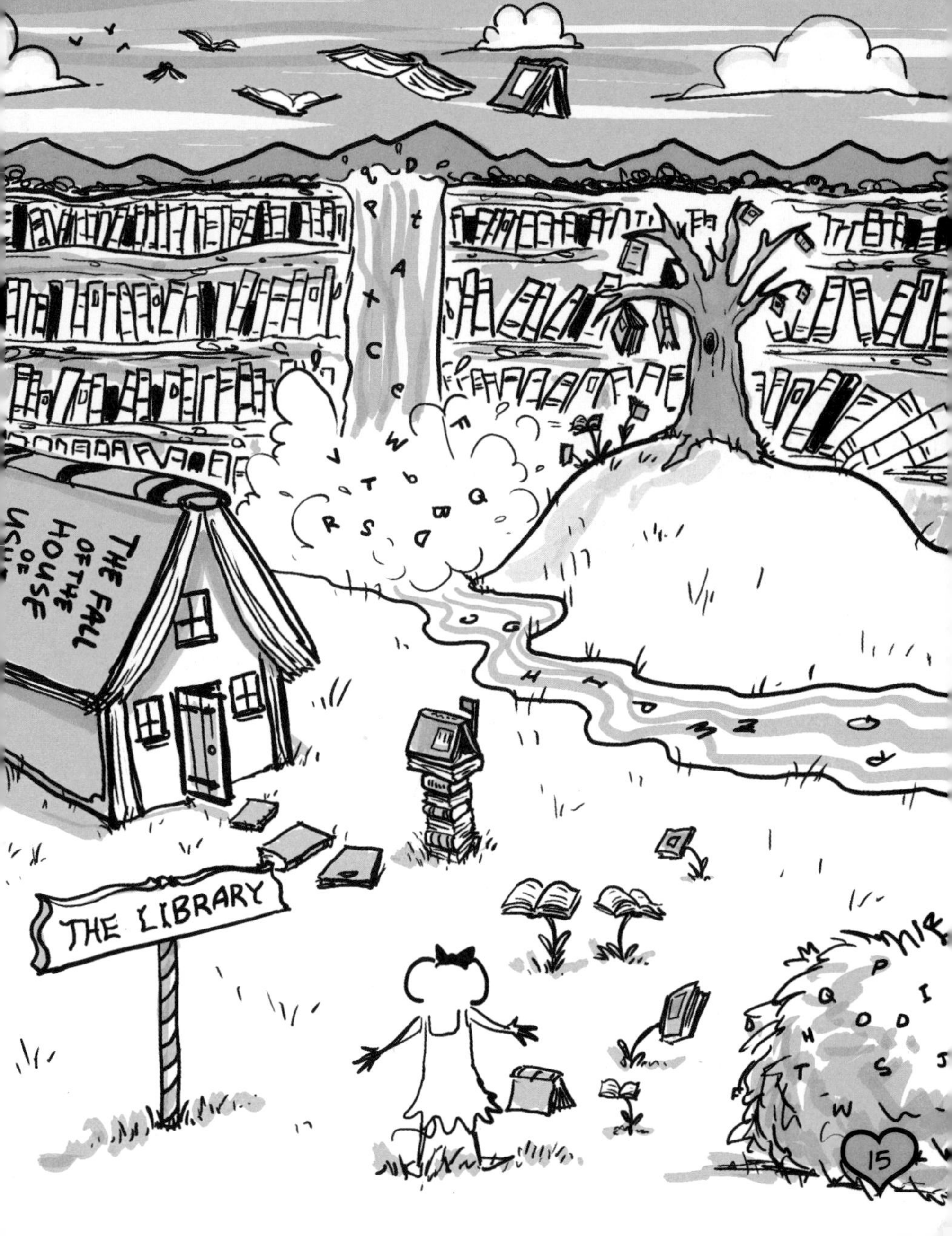
THE FALL OF THE HOUSE OF
THE LIBRARY

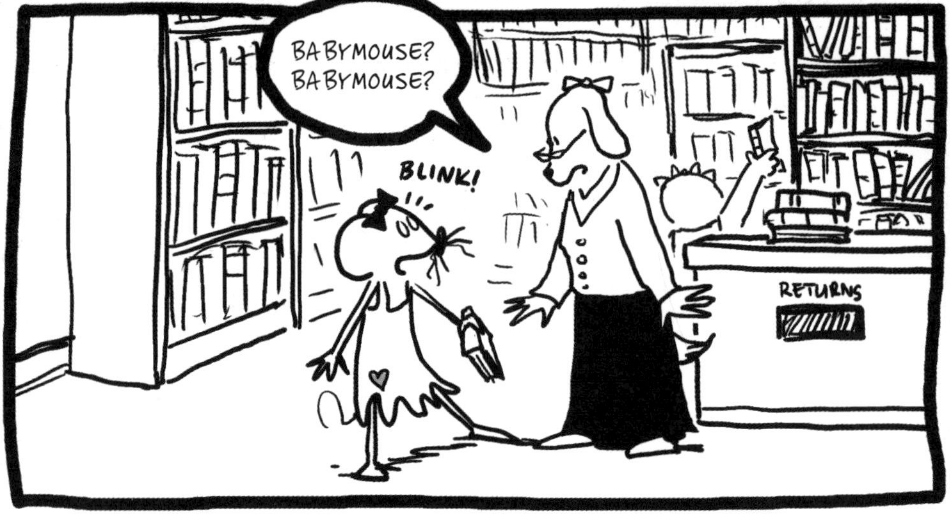
BABYMOUSE? BABYMOUSE?
BLINK!
RETURNS

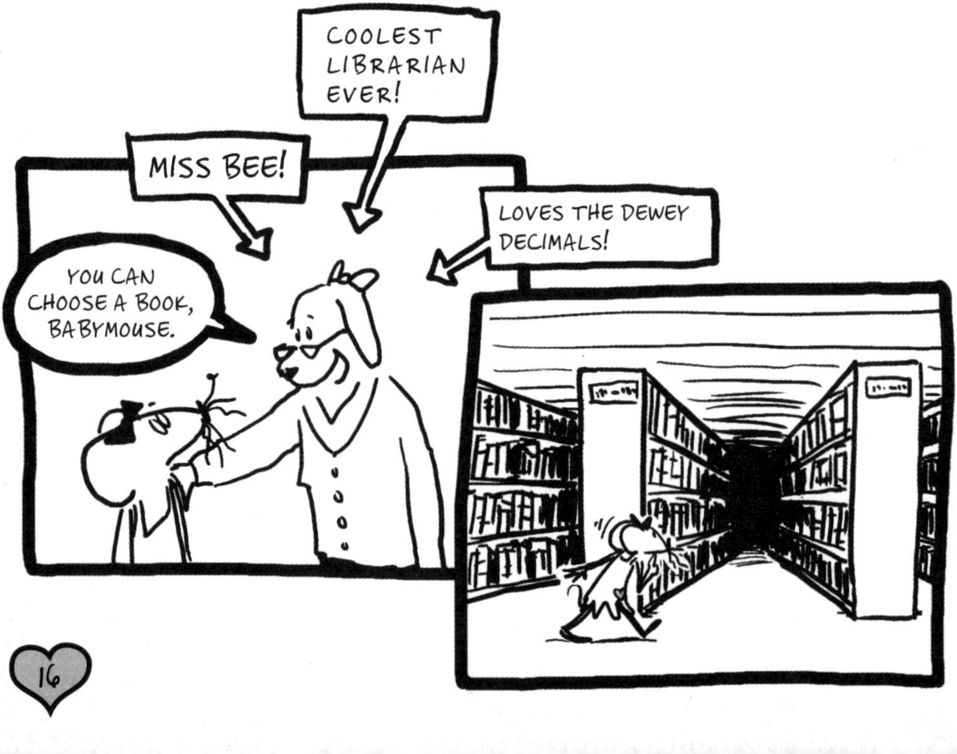
COOLEST LIBRARIAN EVER!
MISS BEE!
LOVES THE DEWEY DECIMALS!
YOU CAN CHOOSE A BOOK, BABYMOUSE.

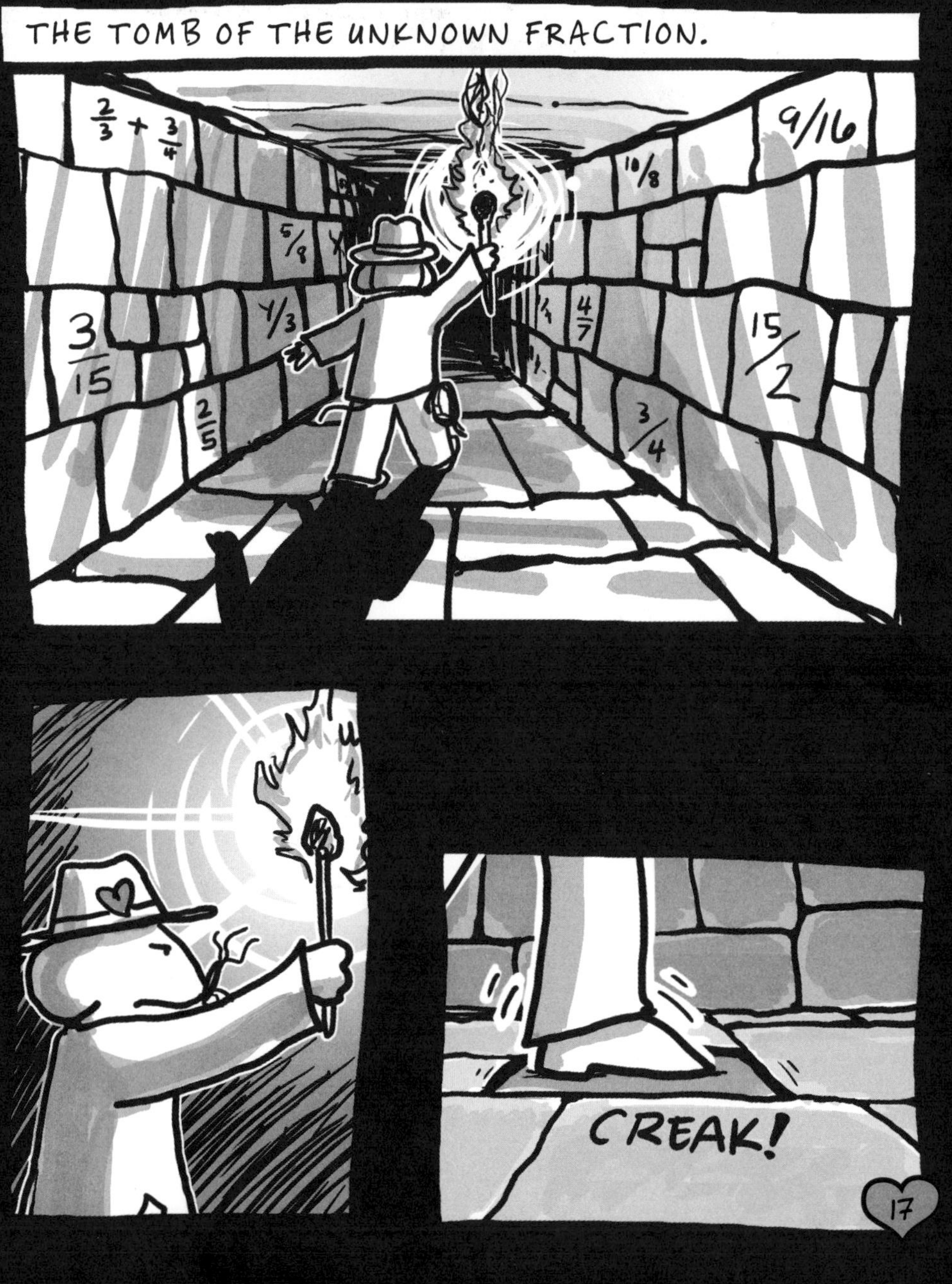
THE TOMB OF THE UNKNOWN FRACTION.
2/3 + 3/4
9/16
10/8
5/8
3/15
1/3
4/7
15/2
2/5
3/4
CREAK!

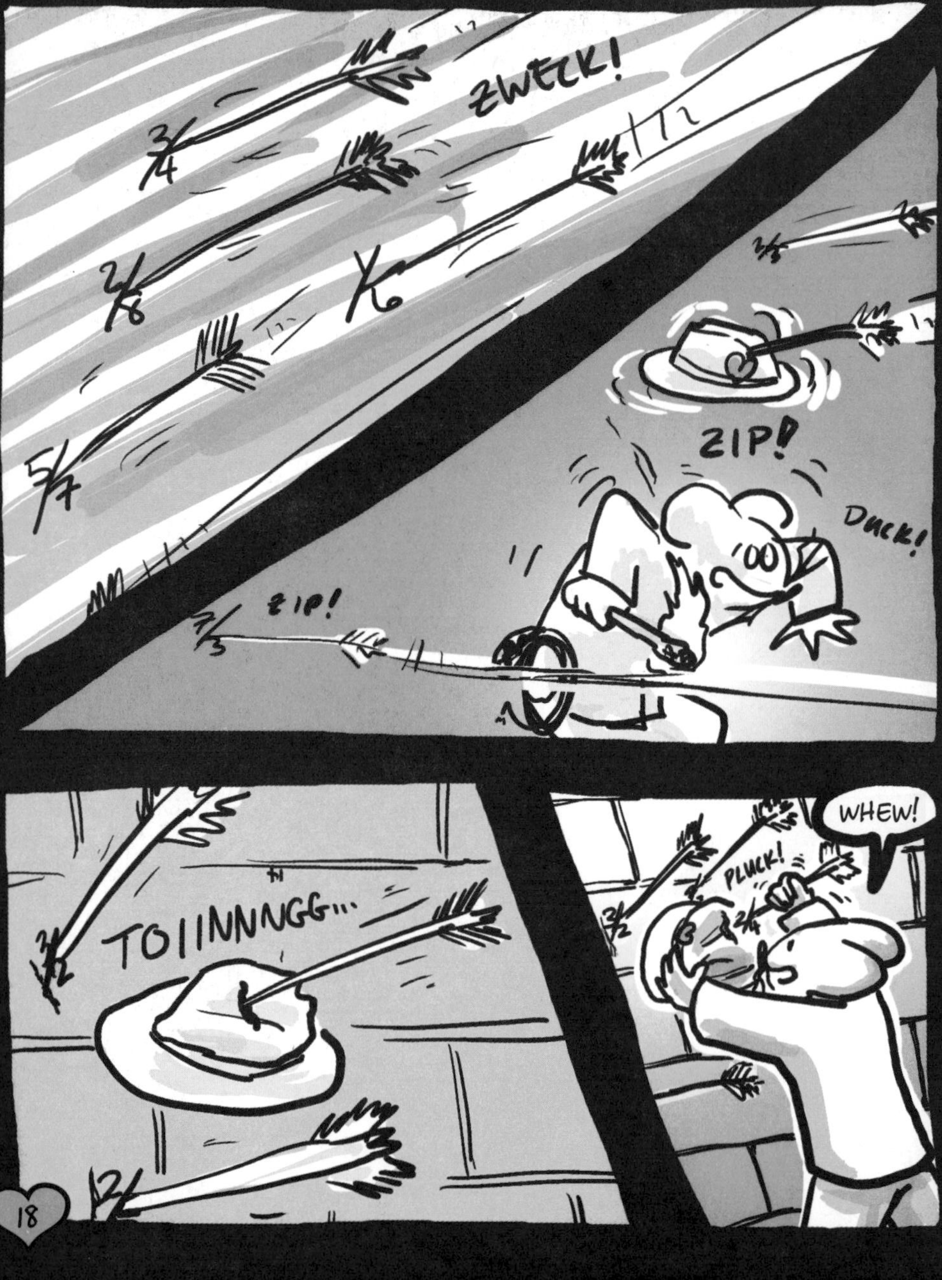
ZWECK!
ZIP!
DUCK!
ZIP!
TOIINNNGG...
WHEW!
PLUCK!

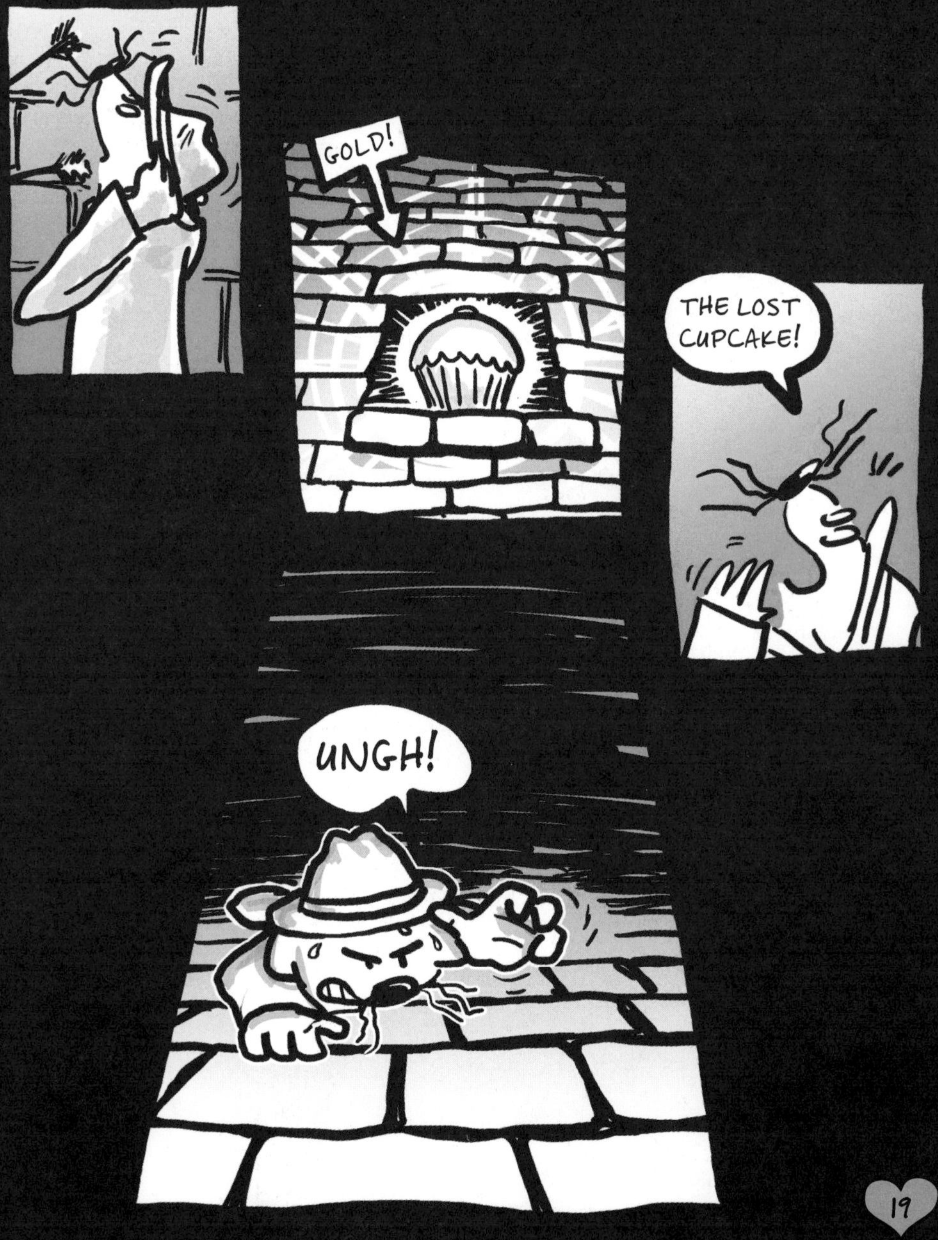
GOLD!
THE LOST CUPCAKE!
UNGH!

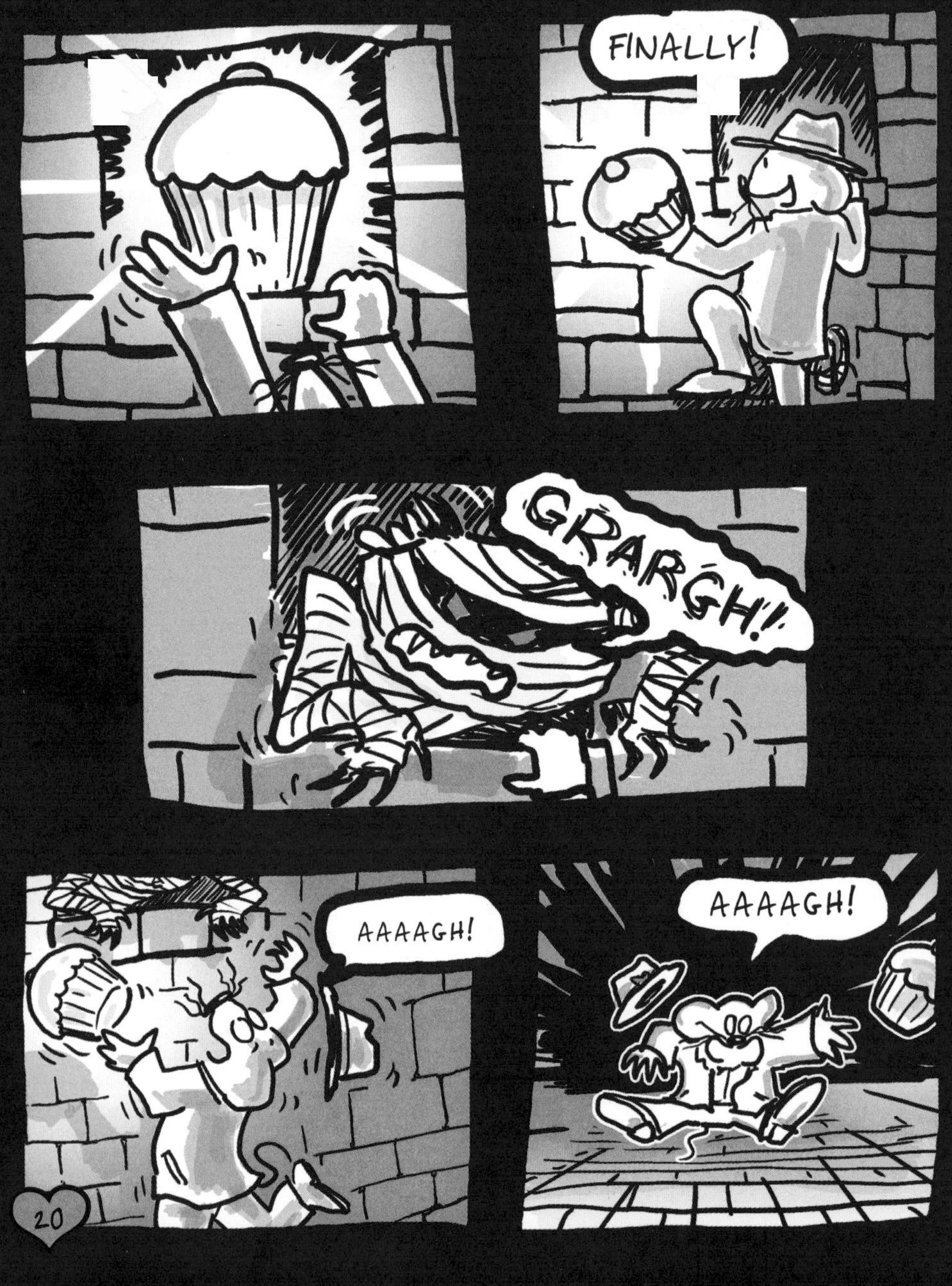
FINALLY!
GRARGH!!
AAAAGH!
AAAAGH!

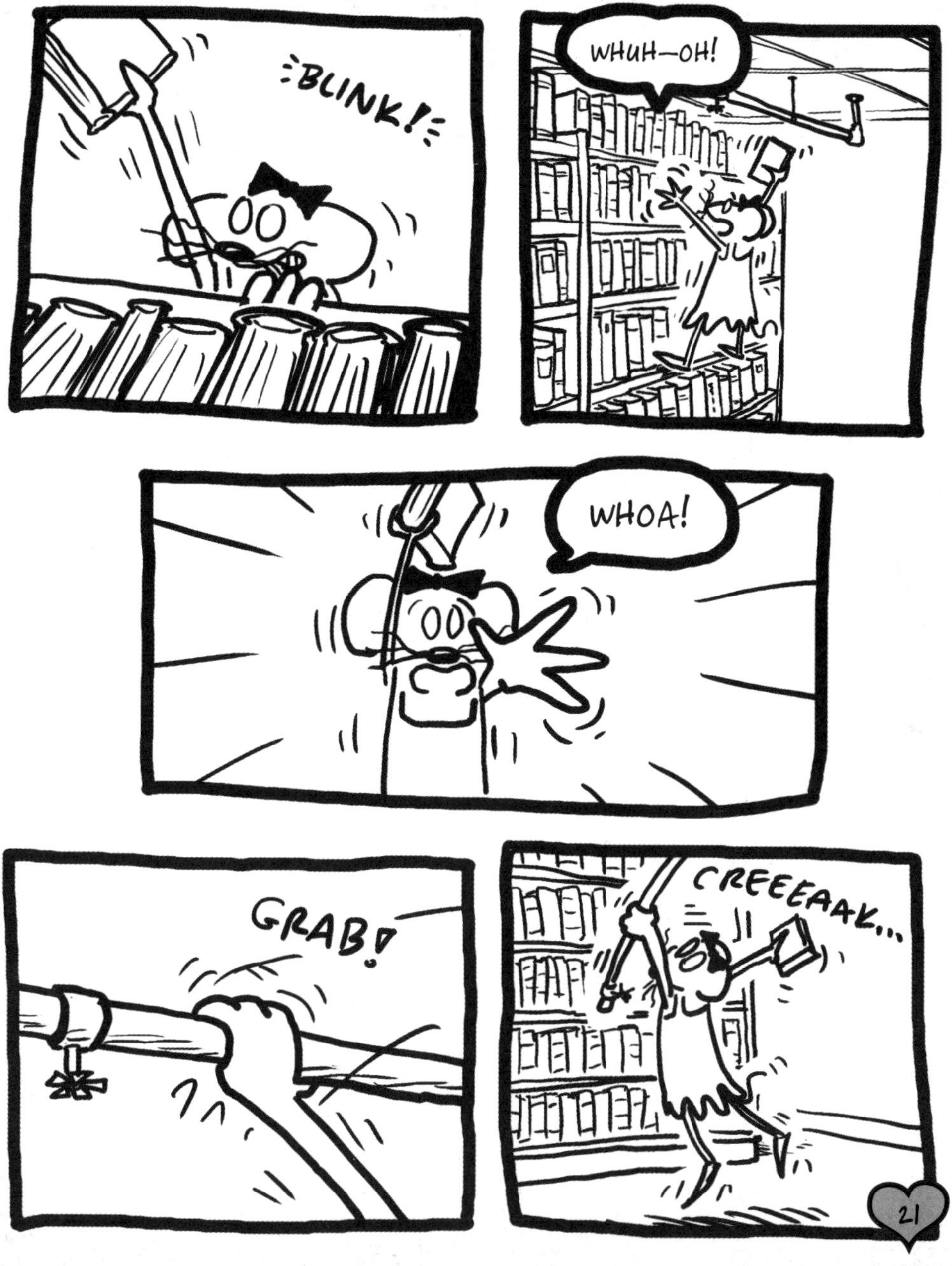
BLINK!
WHUH—OH!
WHOA!
GRAB!
CREEEAAK...

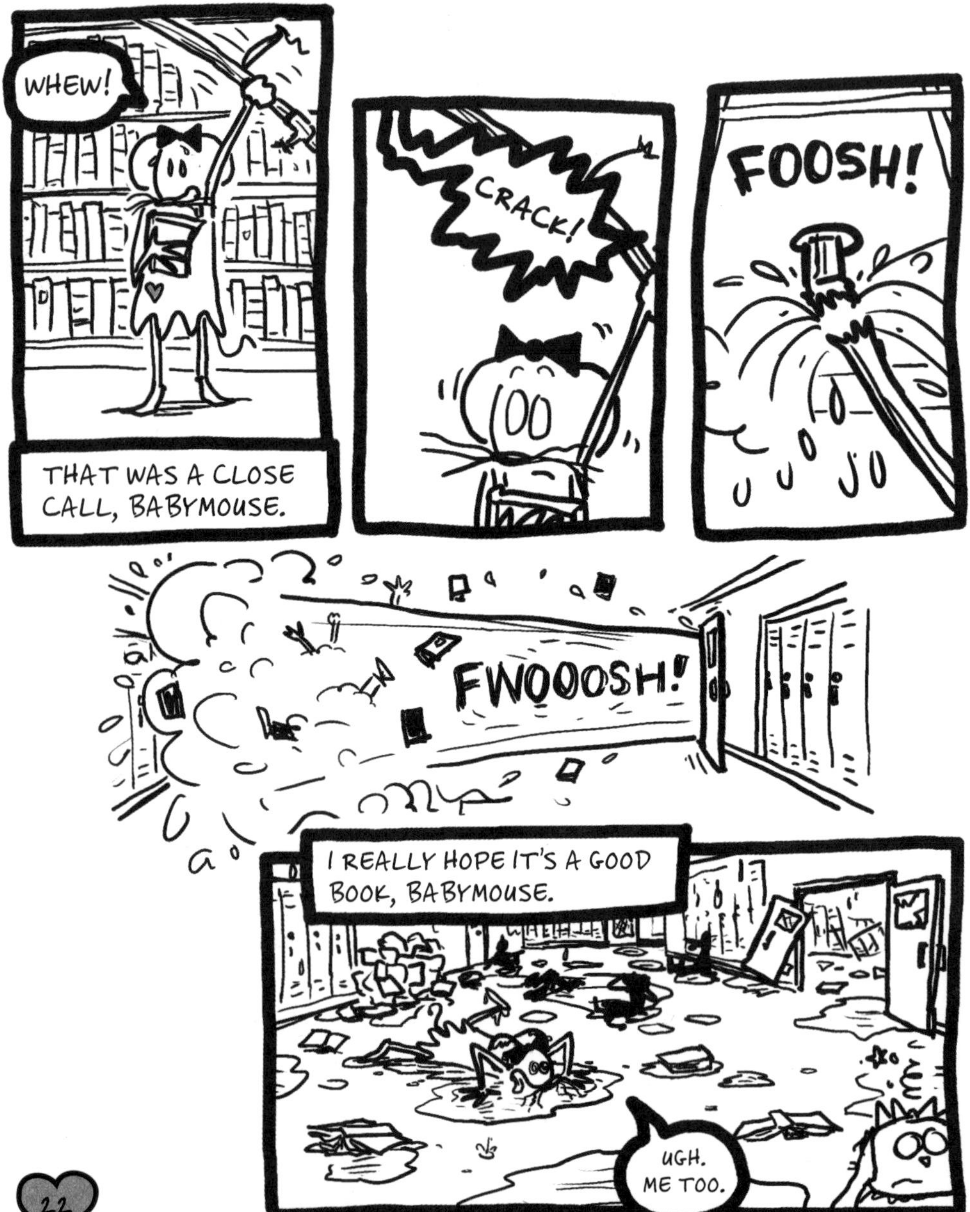
WHEW!
THAT WAS A CLOSE CALL, BABYMOUSE.
CRACK!
FOOSH!
FWOOOSH!
I REALLY HOPE IT'S A GOOD BOOK, BABYMOUSE.
UGH. ME TOO.

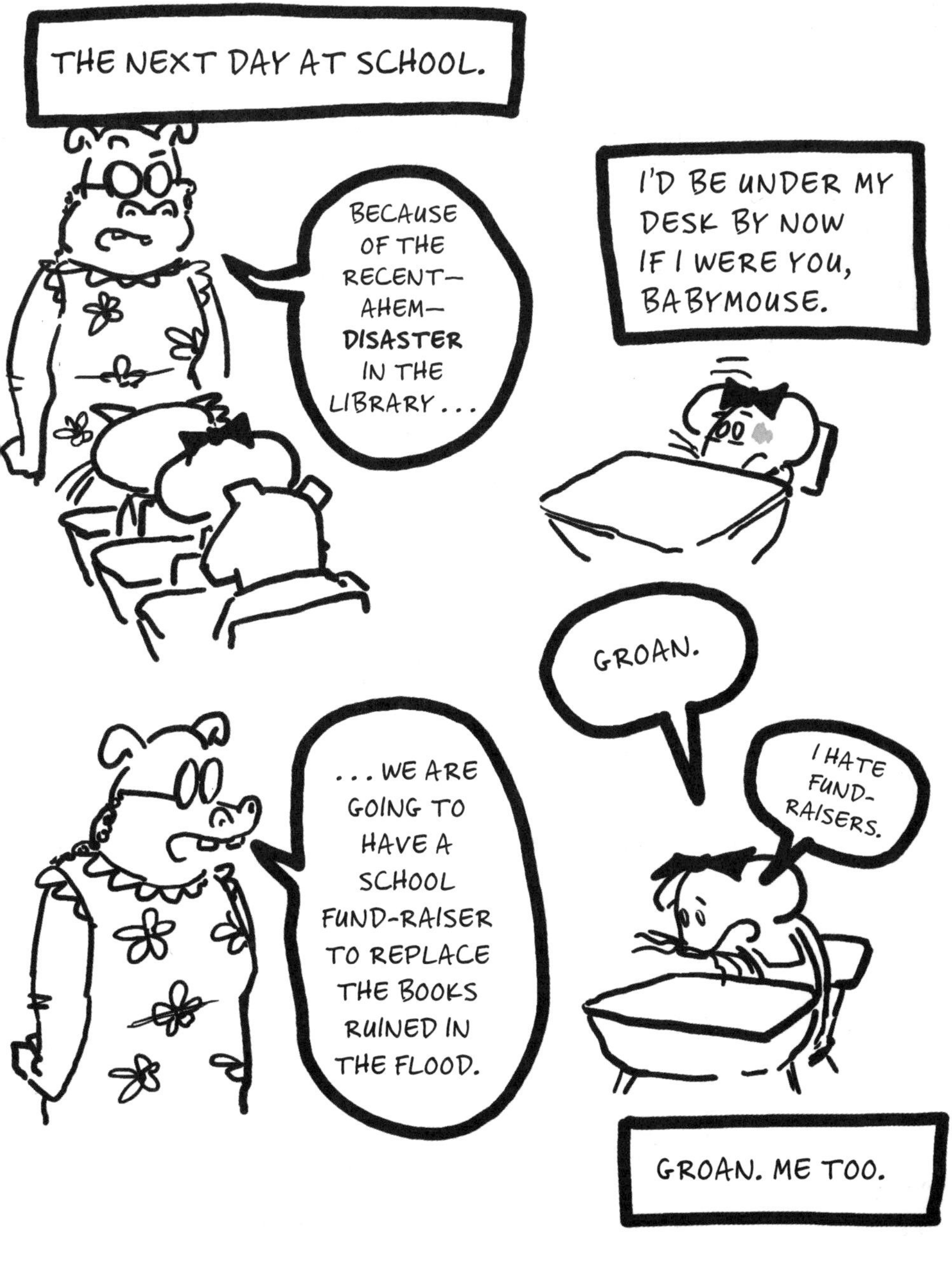
THE NEXT DAY AT SCHOOL.
BECAUSE OF THE RECENT— AHEM— **DISASTER** IN THE LIBRARY . . .
I'D BE UNDER MY DESK BY NOW IF I WERE YOU, BABYMOUSE.
. . . WE ARE GOING TO HAVE A SCHOOL FUND-RAISER TO REPLACE THE BOOKS RUINED IN THE FLOOD.
GROAN.
I HATE FUND-RAISERS.
GROAN. ME TOO.

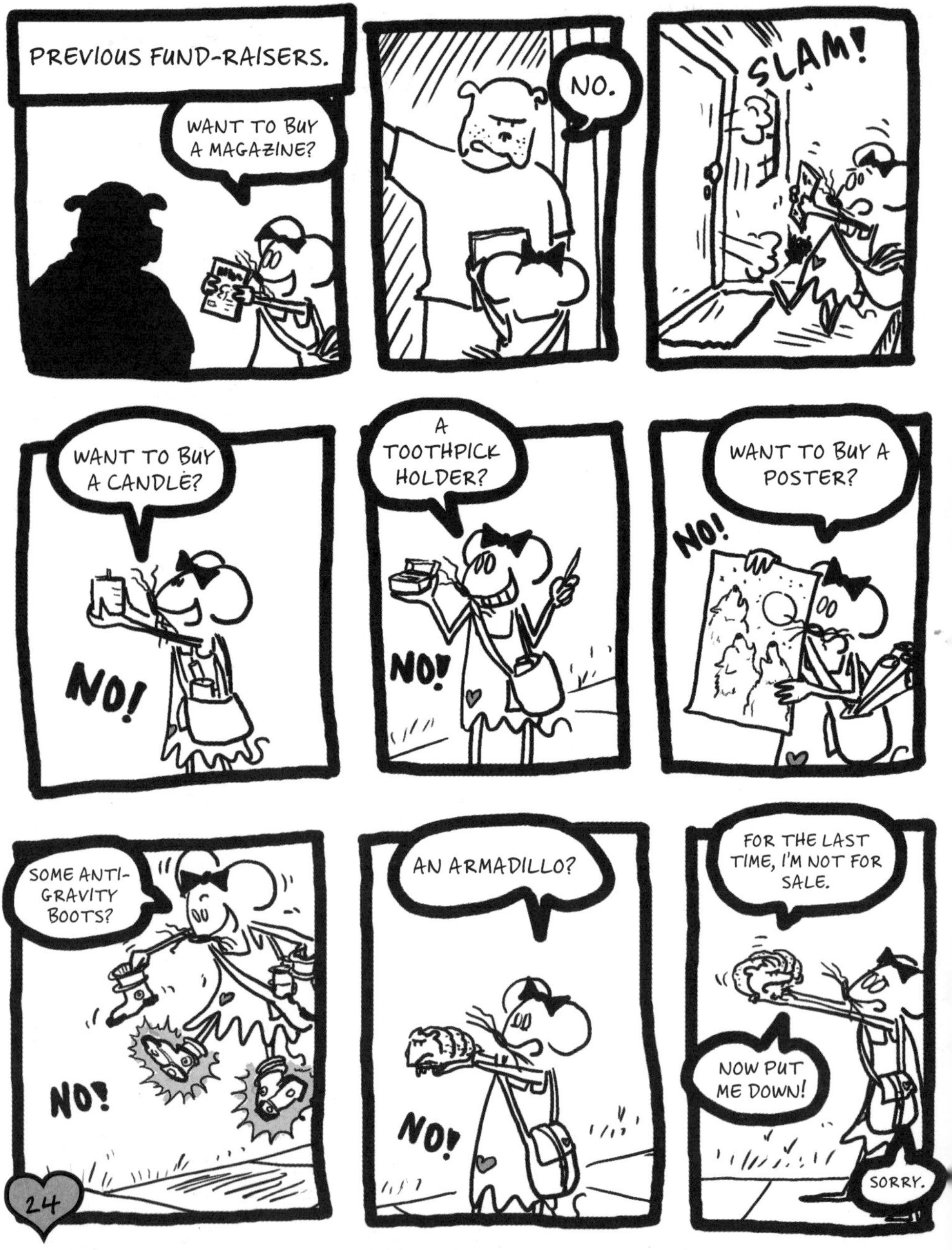

PREVIOUS FUND-RAISERS.
WANT TO BUY A MAGAZINE?
NO.
SLAM!
WANT TO BUY A CANDLE?
NO!
A TOOTHPICK HOLDER?
NO!
WANT TO BUY A POSTER?
NO!
SOME ANTI-GRAVITY BOOTS?
NO!
AN ARMADILLO?
NO!
FOR THE LAST TIME, I'M NOT FOR SALE.
NOW PUT ME DOWN!
SORRY.

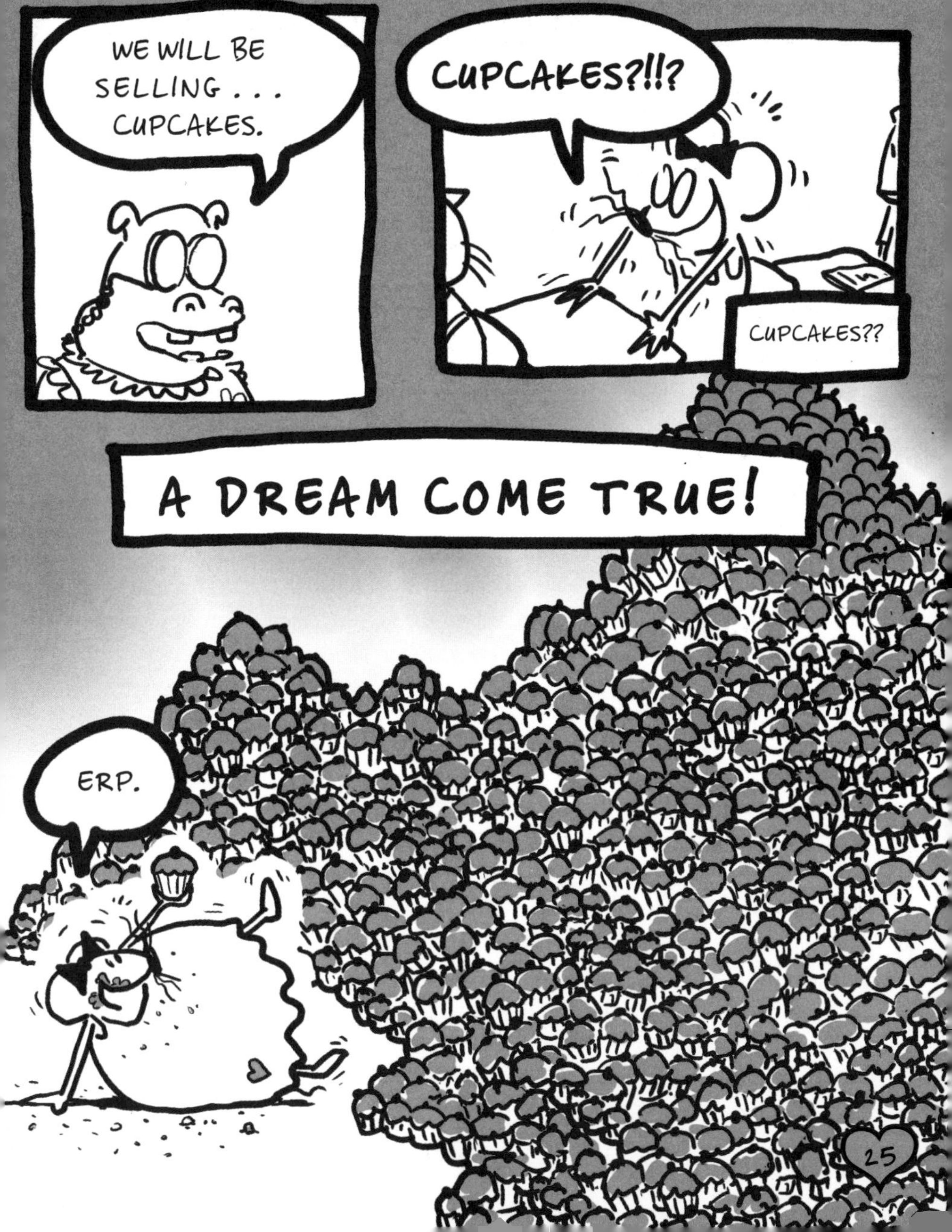
WE WILL BE SELLING . . . CUPCAKES.
CUPCAKES?!!?
CUPCAKES??
A DREAM COME TRUE!
ERP.

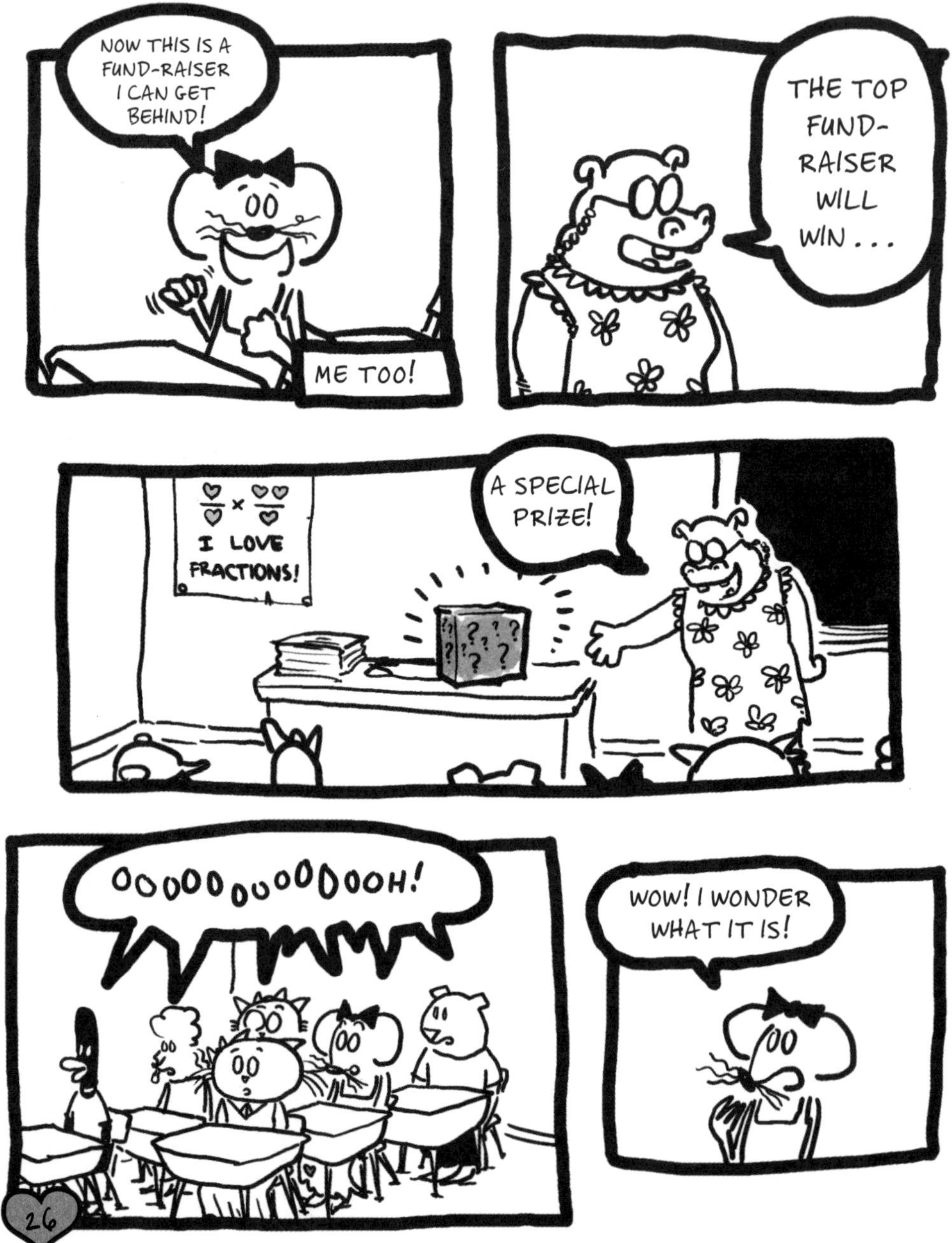
NOW THIS IS A FUND-RAISER I CAN GET BEHIND!
ME TOO!
THE TOP FUND-RAISER WILL WIN . . .
I LOVE FRACTIONS!
A SPECIAL PRIZE!
OOOOOOUOODOOH!
WOW! I WONDER WHAT IT IS!

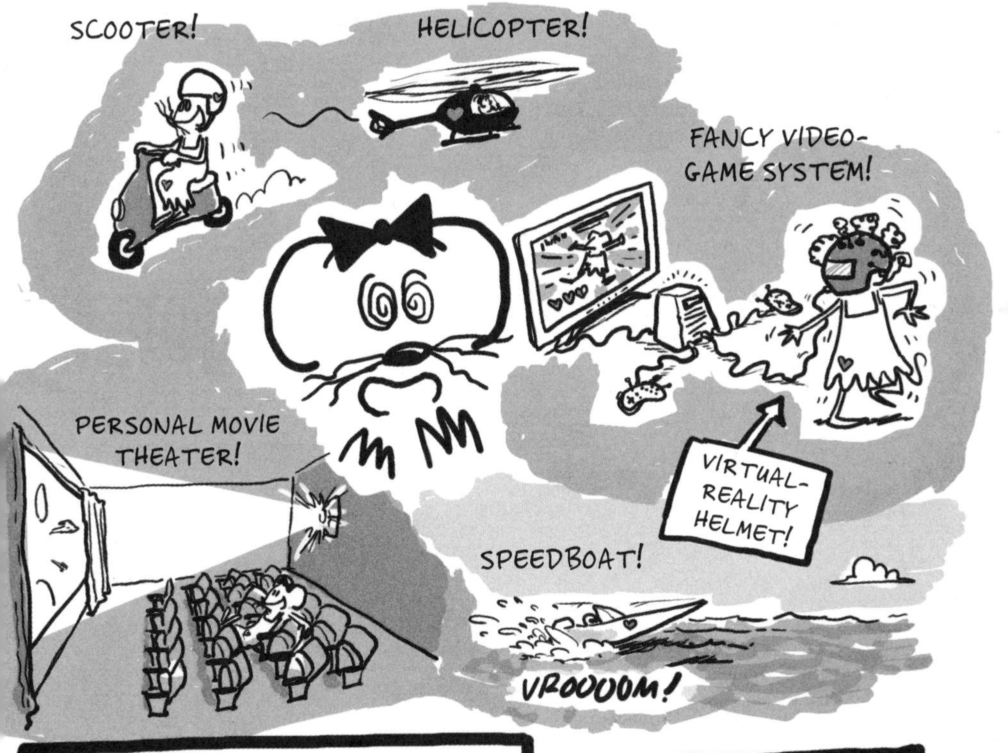
SCOOTER!
HELICOPTER!
FANCY VIDEO-GAME SYSTEM!
PERSONAL MOVIE THEATER!
VIRTUAL-REALITY HELMET!
SPEEDBOAT!
VROOOOOM!

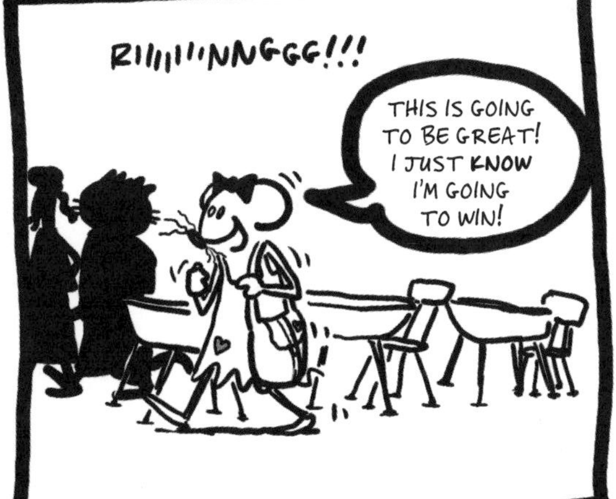
RIIIIII'NNGGG!!!
THIS IS GOING TO BE GREAT! I JUST **KNOW** I'M GOING TO WIN!

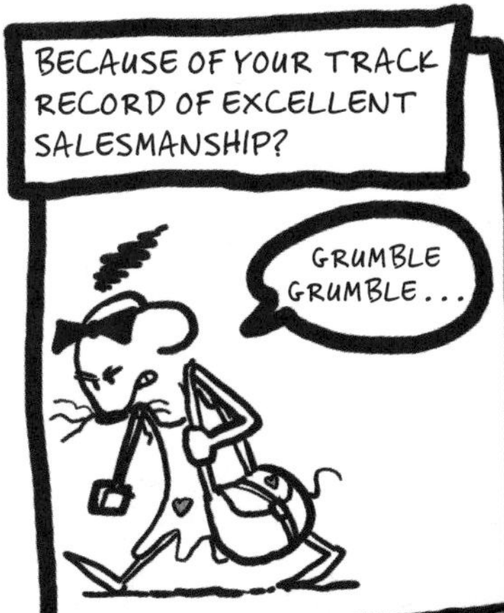
BECAUSE OF YOUR TRACK RECORD OF EXCELLENT SALESMANSHIP?
GRUMBLE GRUMBLE...

END OF THE DAY.

RIIINGGG!!!

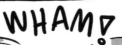

WHAM!

PANT
PANT

RRRRRUUUMMMMBBLE...

28

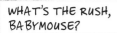 WHAT'S THE RUSH, BABYMOUSE?

HUFF! HUFF! HAVE TO—HUFF!—HURRY HOME AND—PUFF!—START SELLING BEFORE THE OTHER KIDS—PUFF!—GET TO THE NEIGHBORHOOD! PUFF!

ZIP!

THUNK!

ZIP!

SNATCH!

WOLF!

MUNCH MUNCH

SLURP!

HOW WAS SCHOOL, BABYMOUSE—?

CAN'T TALK! GOTTA SELL!

SWISH!

29

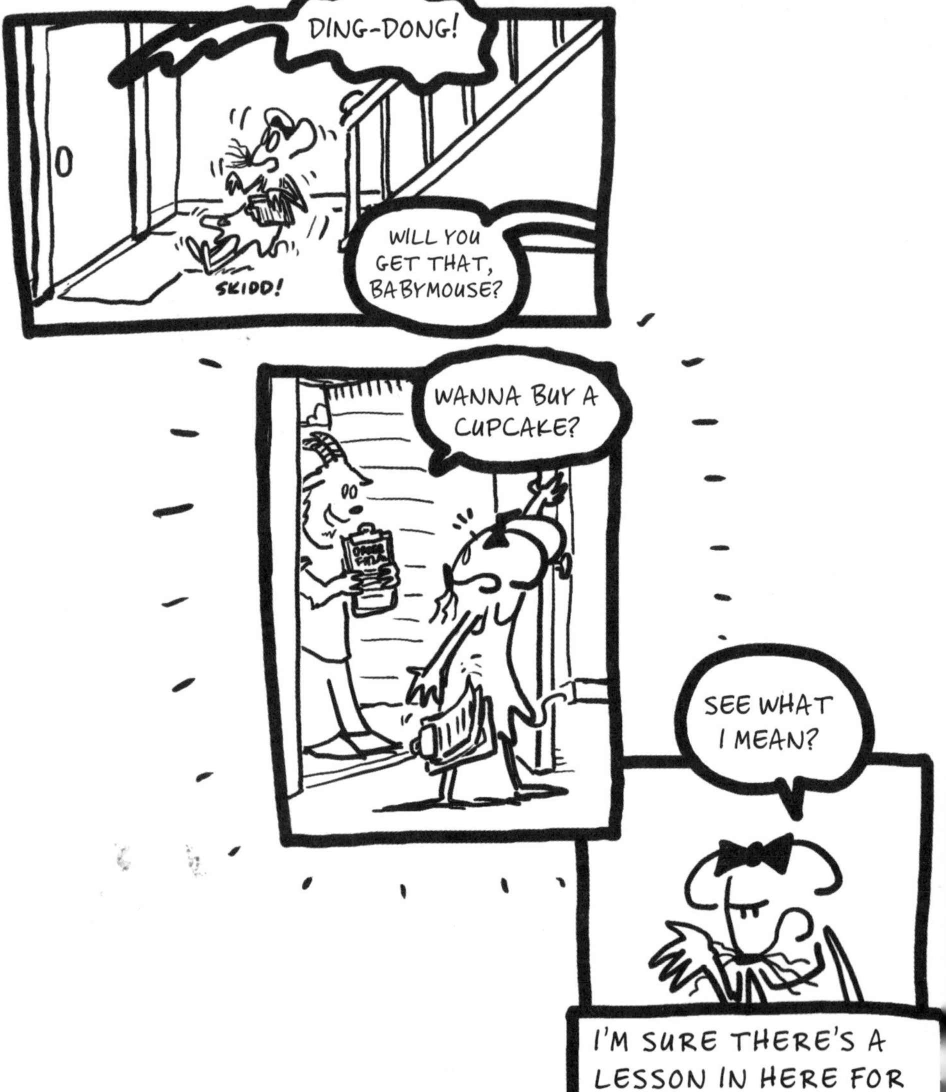
DING-DONG!
SKIDD!
WILL YOU GET THAT, BABYMOUSE?
WANNA BUY A CUPCAKE?
SEE WHAT I MEAN?
I'M SURE THERE'S A LESSON IN HERE FOR THE ECONOMISTS.

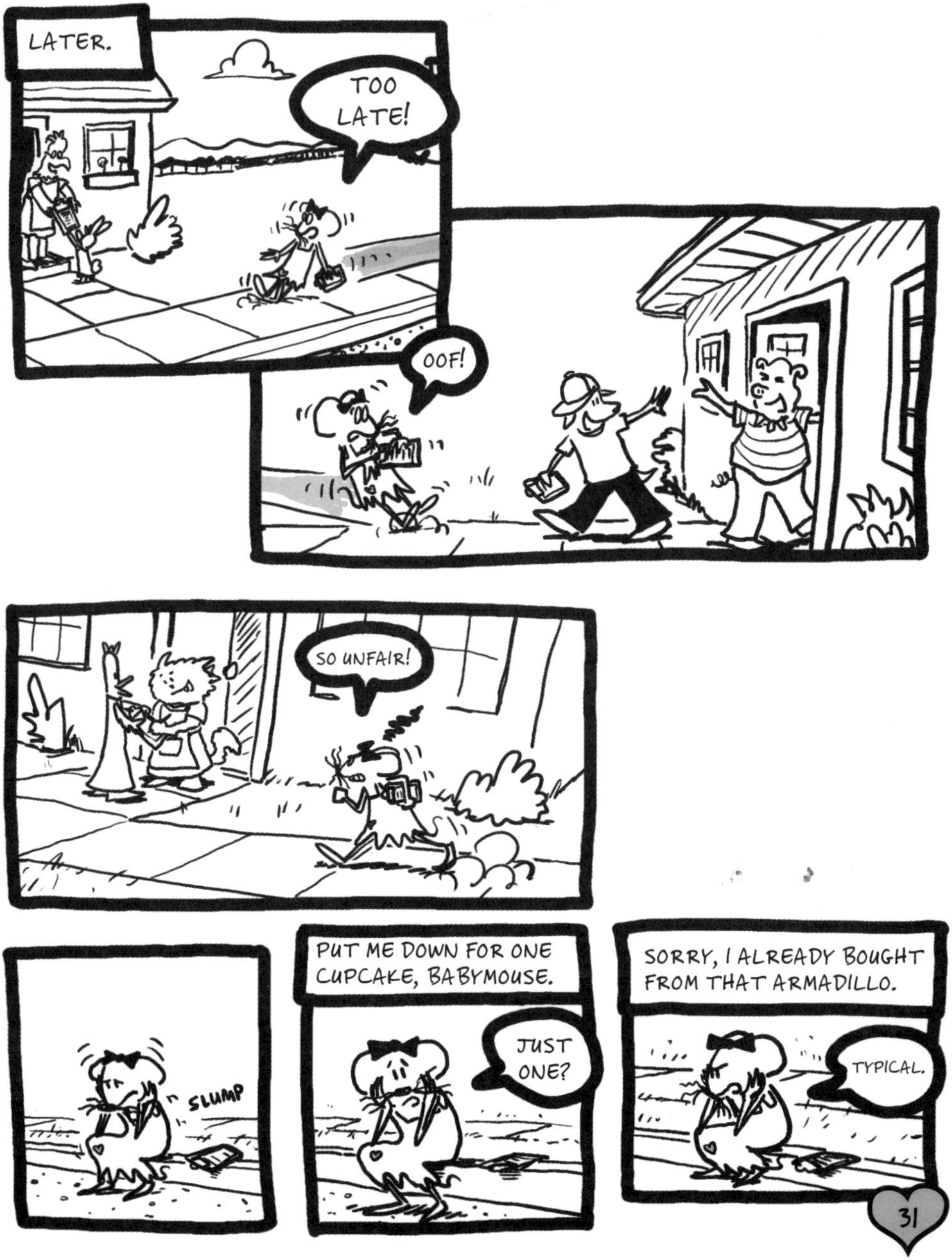
LATER.
TOO LATE!
OOF!
SO UNFAIR!
SLUMP
PUT ME DOWN FOR ONE CUPCAKE, BABYMOUSE.
JUST ONE?
SORRY, I ALREADY BOUGHT FROM THAT ARMADILLO.
TYPICAL.

HOW ARE THE CUPCAKE SALES GOING, BABYMOUSE?

NOT GOOD. THERE'RE TOO MANY KIDS IN THE NEIGHBORHOOD.

SHRUG

WHAT ABOUT FAMILY?

YOU WANT TO BUY SOME CUPCAKES?

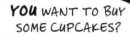

I'LL BUY A FEW, BABYMOUSE. BUT WHAT I MEAN IS, WHY DON'T YOU ASK SOME RELATIVES?

THAT'S A GREAT IDEA!

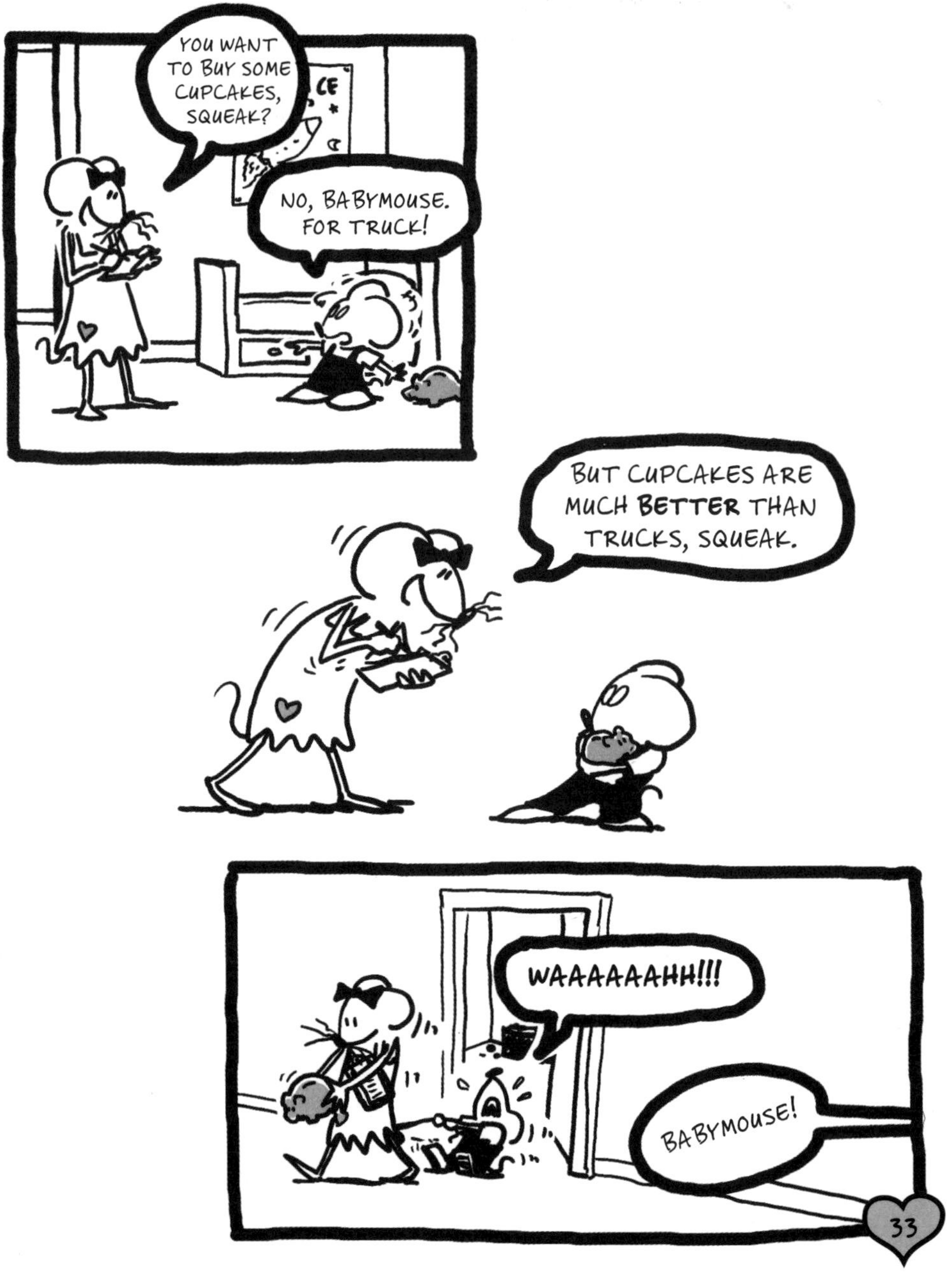
YOU WANT TO BUY SOME CUPCAKES, SQUEAK?
NO, BABYMOUSE. FOR TRUCK!
BUT CUPCAKES ARE MUCH **BETTER** THAN TRUCKS, SQUEAK.
WAAAAAAHH!!!
BABYMOUSE!

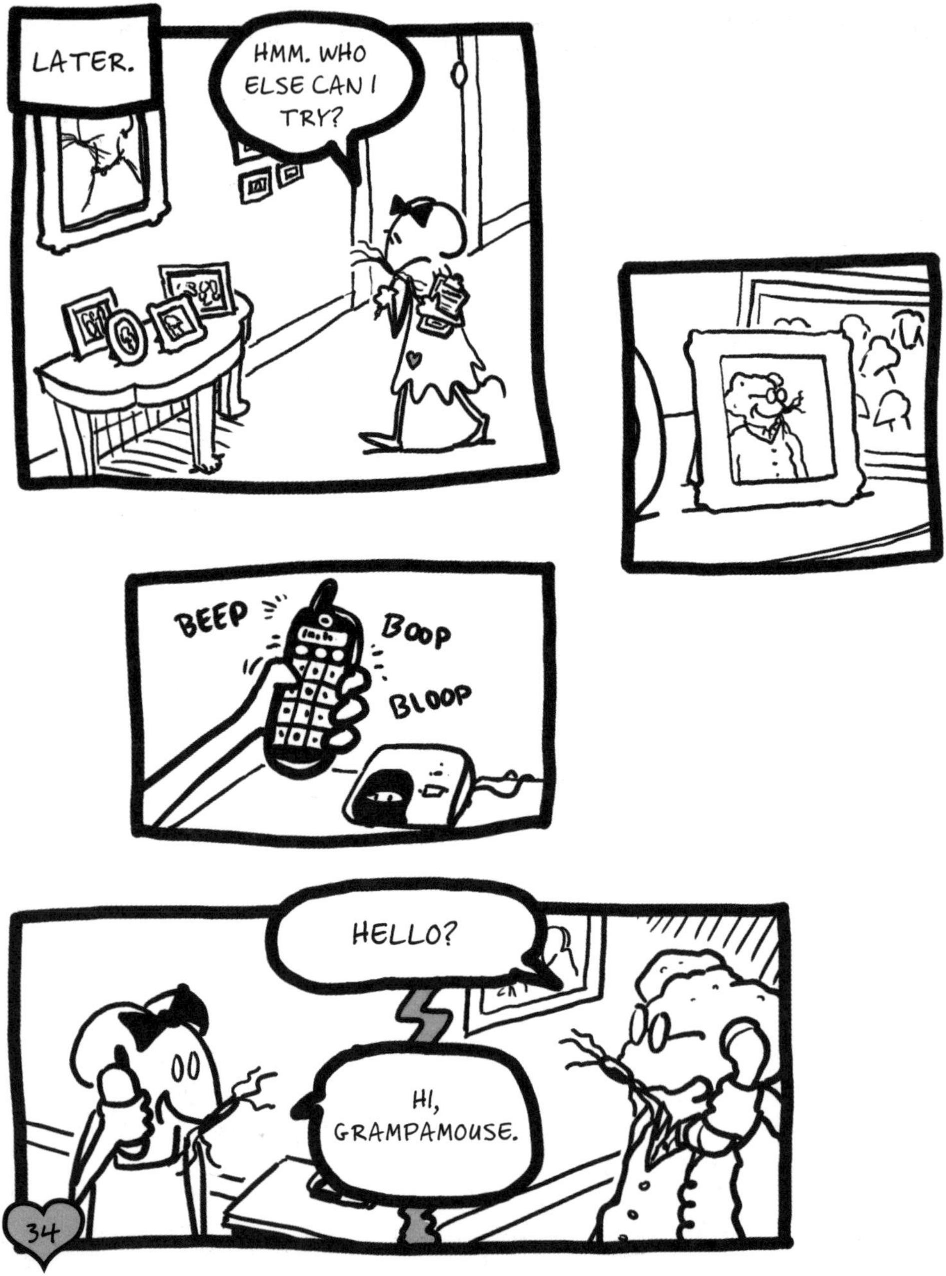
LATER.
HMM. WHO ELSE CAN I TRY?
BEEP
BOOP
BLOOP
HELLO?
HI, GRAMPAMOUSE.

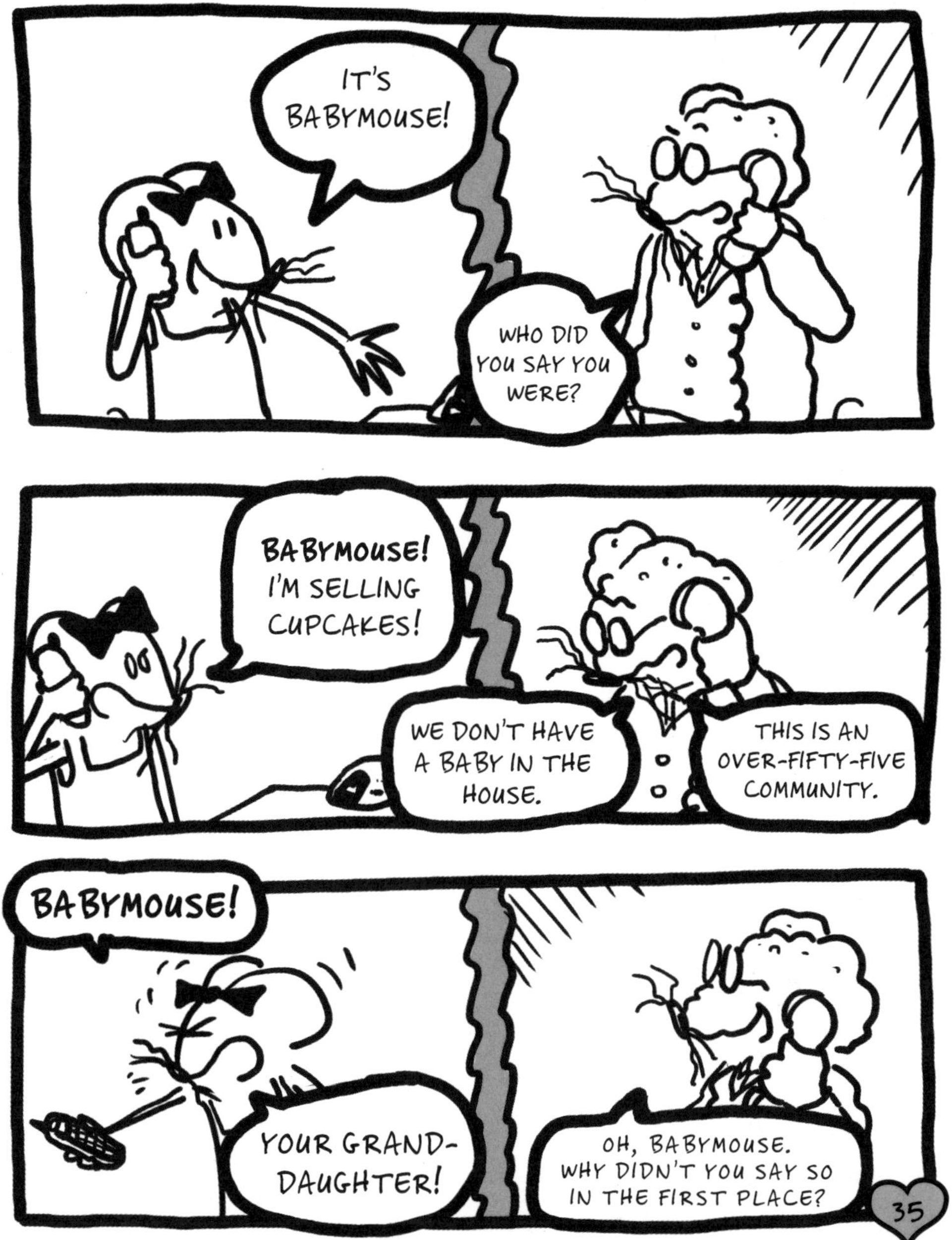
IT'S BABYMOUSE!
WHO DID YOU SAY YOU WERE?
BABYMOUSE! I'M SELLING CUPCAKES!
WE DON'T HAVE A BABY IN THE HOUSE.
THIS IS AN OVER-FIFTY-FIVE COMMUNITY.
BABYMOUSE!
YOUR GRAND-DAUGHTER!
OH, BABYMOUSE. WHY DIDN'T YOU SAY SO IN THE FIRST PLACE?

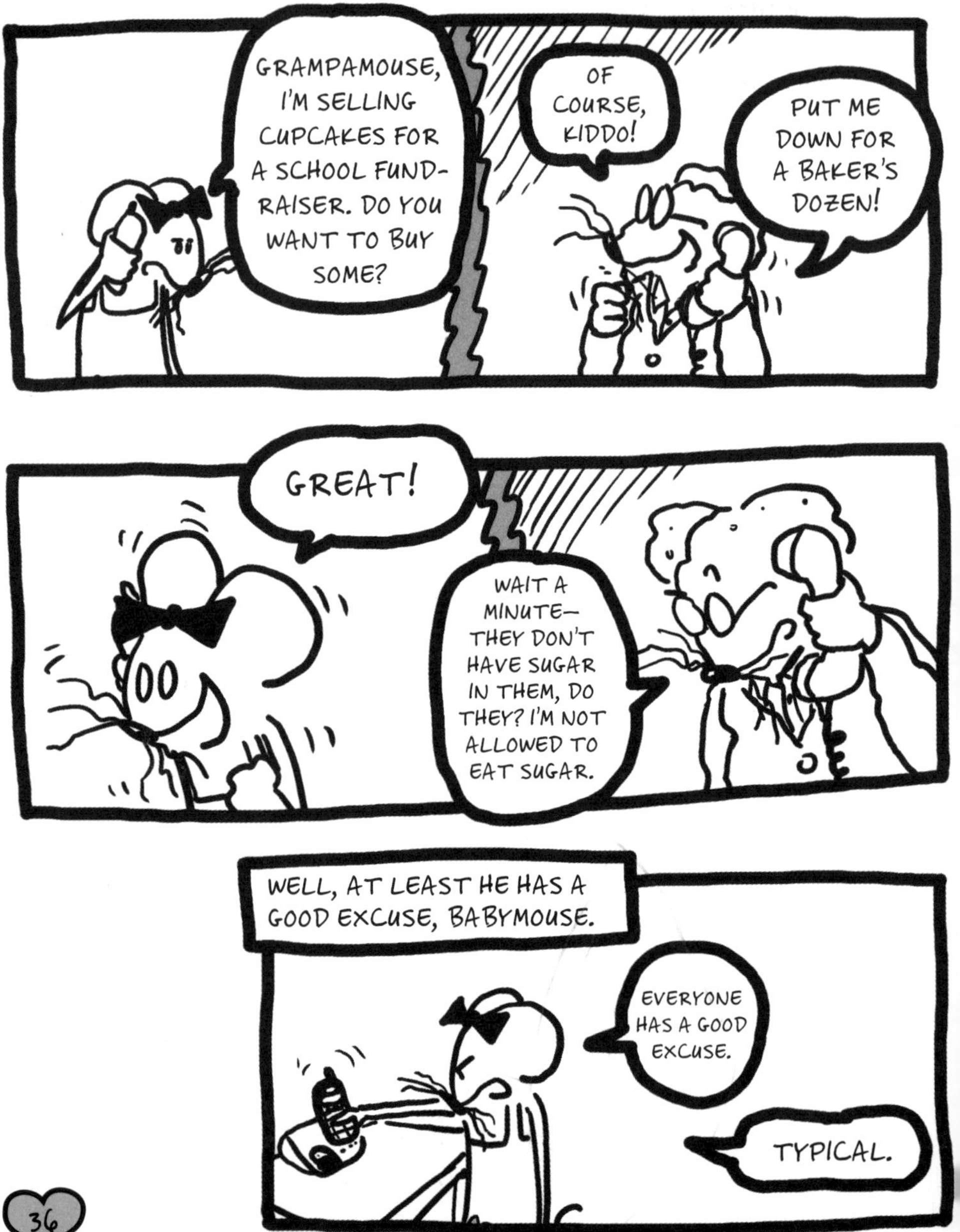
GRAMPAMOUSE, I'M SELLING CUPCAKES FOR A SCHOOL FUND-RAISER. DO YOU WANT TO BUY SOME?
OF COURSE, KIDDO!
PUT ME DOWN FOR A BAKER'S DOZEN!
GREAT!
WAIT A MINUTE— THEY DON'T HAVE SUGAR IN THEM, DO THEY? I'M NOT ALLOWED TO EAT SUGAR.
WELL, AT LEAST HE HAS A GOOD EXCUSE, BABYMOUSE.
EVERYONE HAS A GOOD EXCUSE.
TYPICAL.

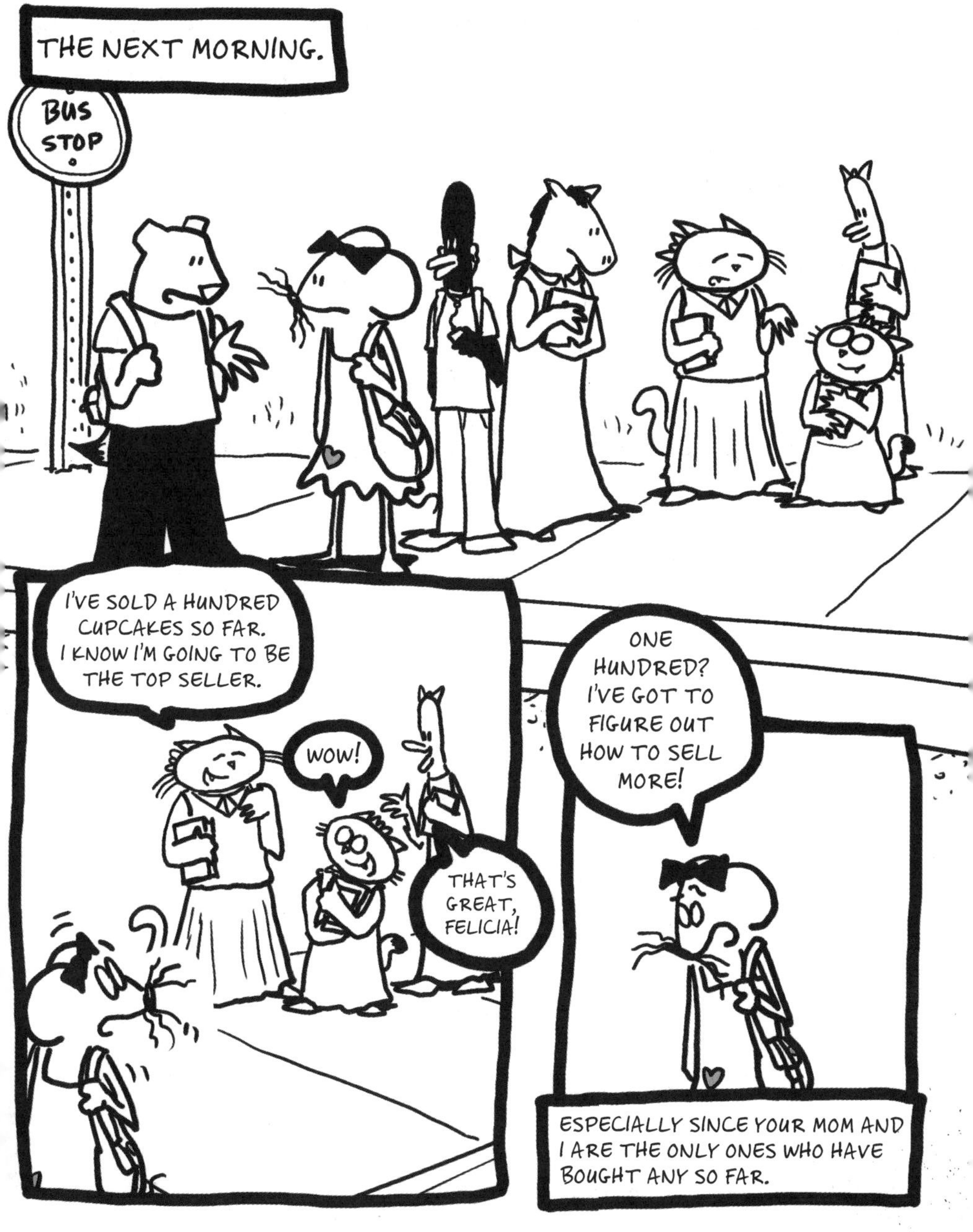
THE NEXT MORNING.
BUS STOP
I'VE SOLD A HUNDRED CUPCAKES SO FAR. I KNOW I'M GOING TO BE THE TOP SELLER.
WOW!
THAT'S GREAT, FELICIA!
ONE HUNDRED? I'VE GOT TO FIGURE OUT HOW TO SELL MORE!
ESPECIALLY SINCE YOUR MOM AND I ARE THE ONLY ONES WHO HAVE BOUGHT ANY SO FAR.

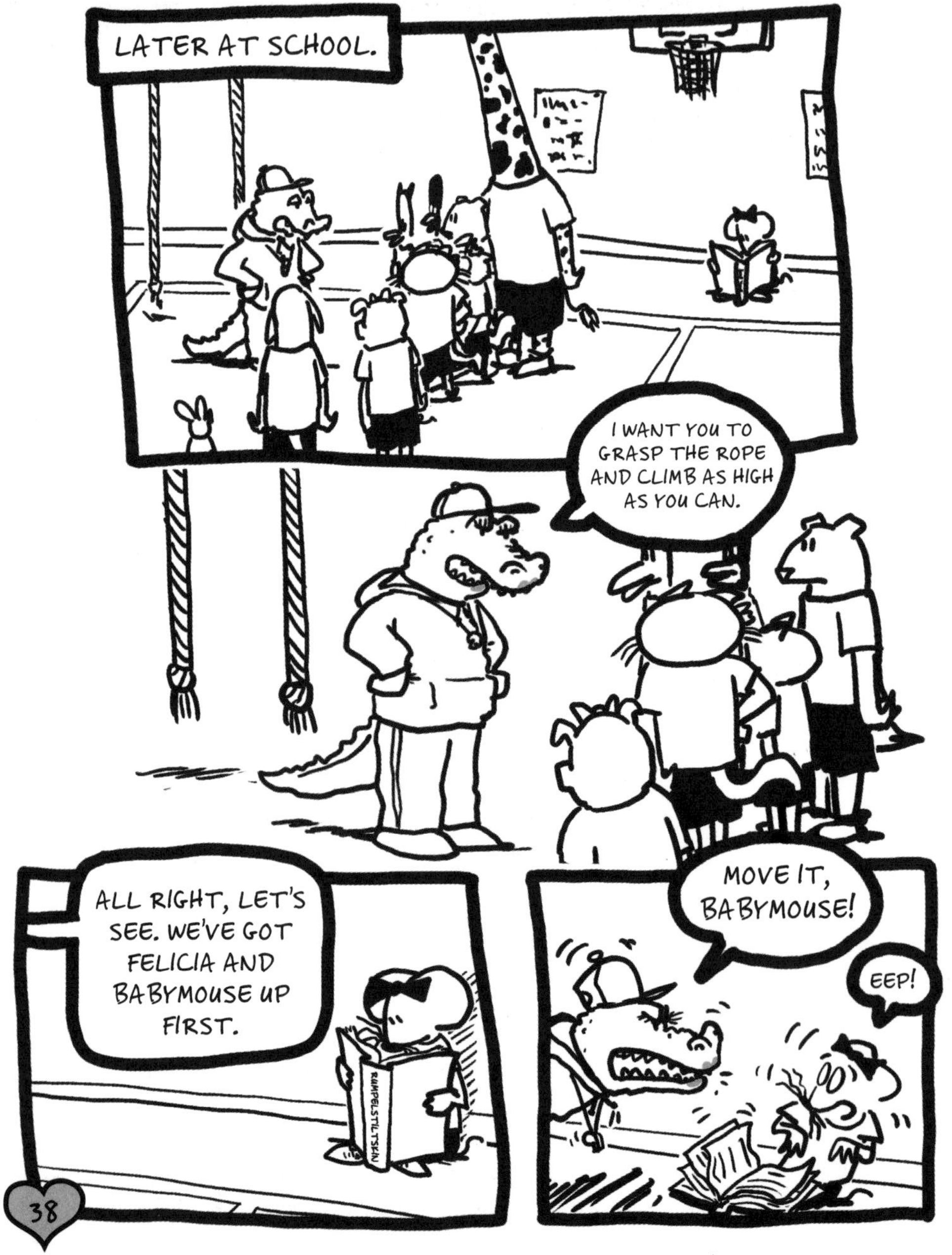

LATER AT SCHOOL.
I WANT YOU TO GRASP THE ROPE AND CLIMB AS HIGH AS YOU CAN.
ALL RIGHT, LET'S SEE. WE'VE GOT FELICIA AND BABYMOUSE UP FIRST.
RUMPELSTILTSKIN
MOVE IT, BABYMOUSE!
EEP!

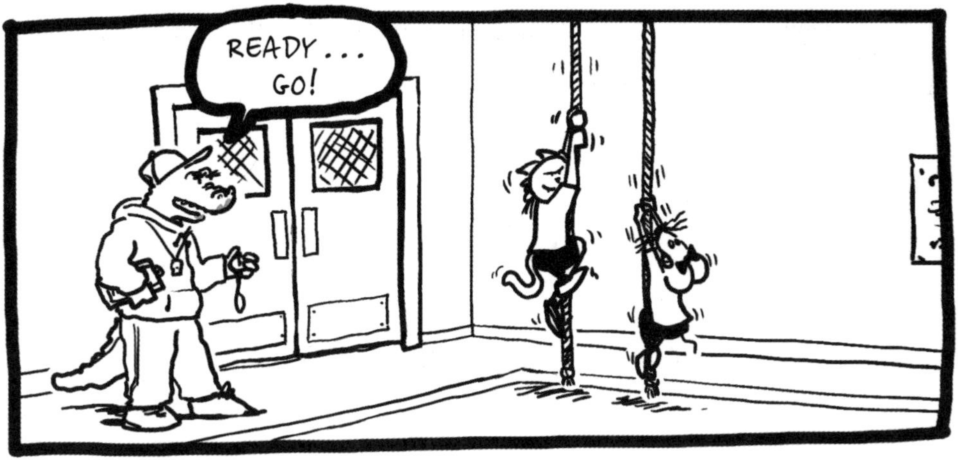
READY . . .
GO!

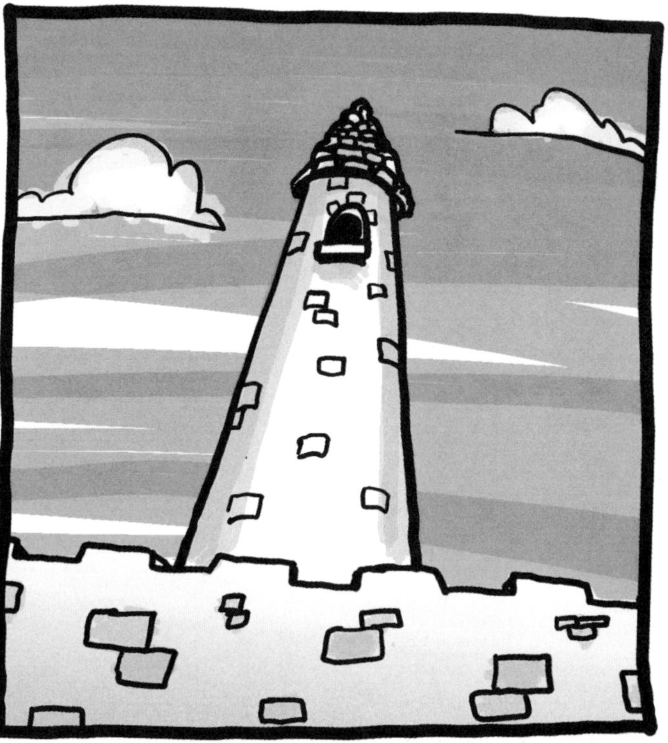

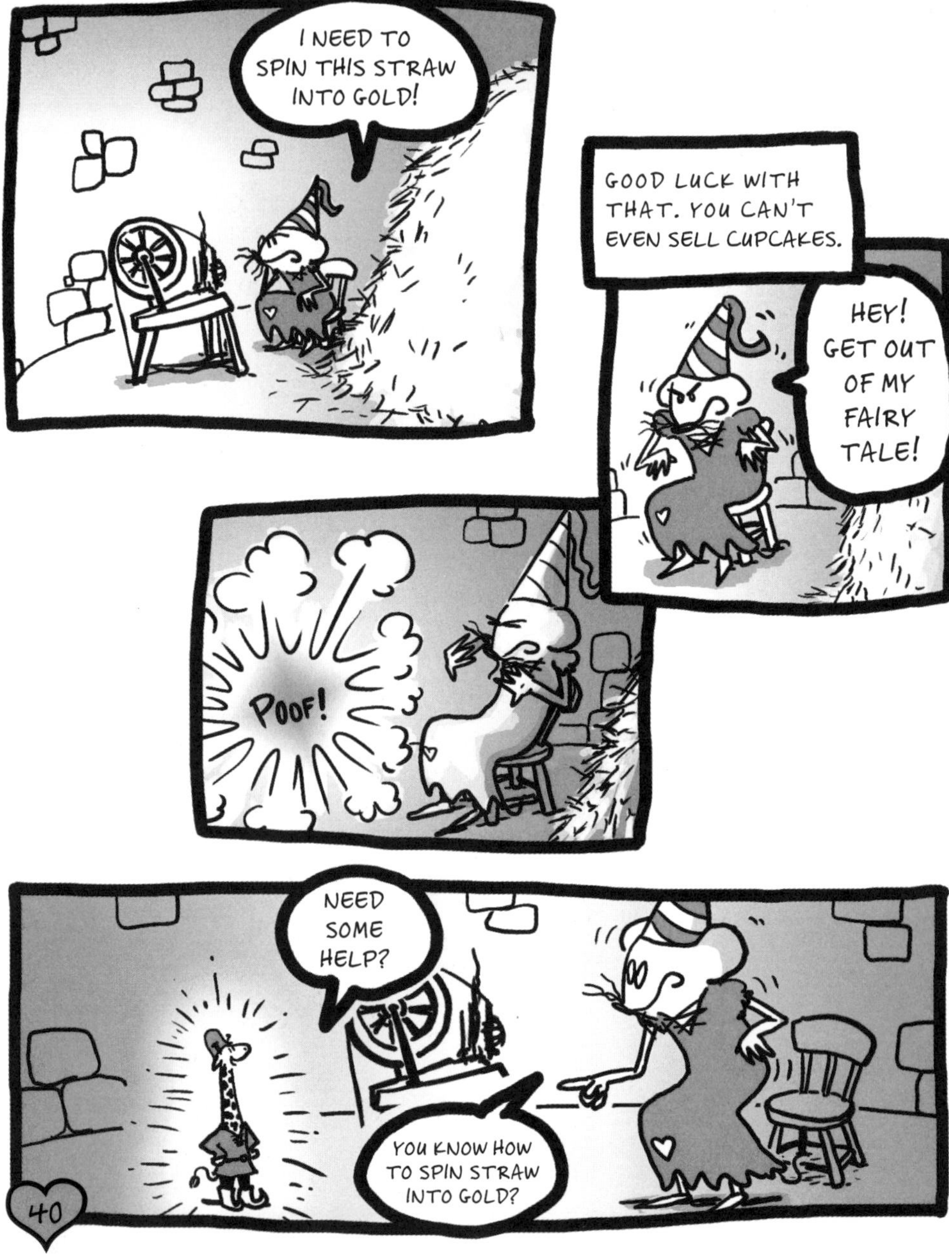
I NEED TO SPIN THIS STRAW INTO GOLD!
GOOD LUCK WITH THAT. YOU CAN'T EVEN SELL CUPCAKES.
HEY! GET OUT OF MY FAIRY TALE!
POOF!
NEED SOME HELP?
YOU KNOW HOW TO SPIN STRAW INTO GOLD?

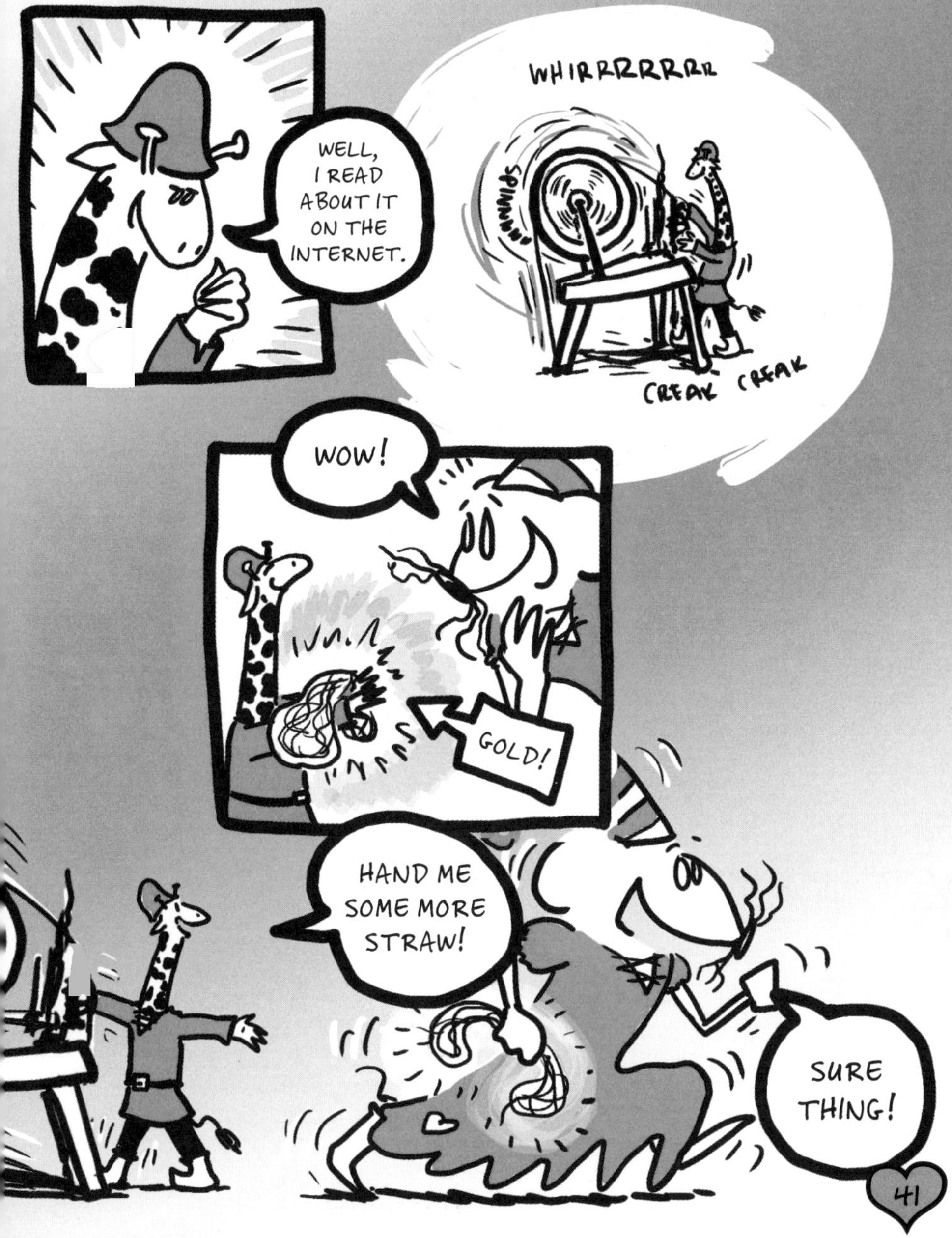
WELL, I READ ABOUT IT ON THE INTERNET.
WHIRRRRRRR
SPINNNN
CREAK CREAK
WOW!
GOLD!
HAND ME SOME MORE STRAW!
SURE THING!

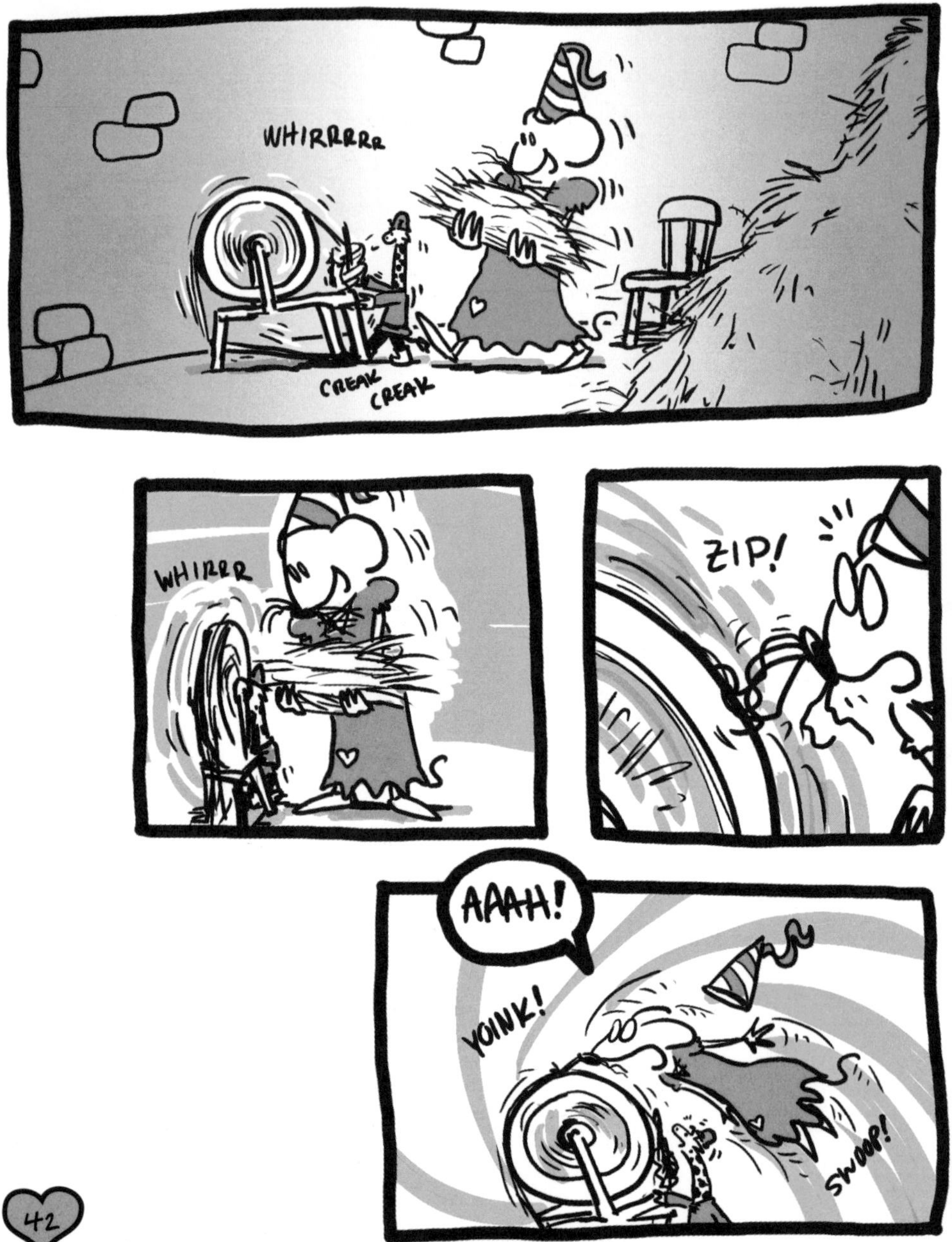
WHIRRRRR
CREAK
CREAK
WHIRRR
ZIP!
AAAH!
YOINK!
SWOOP!

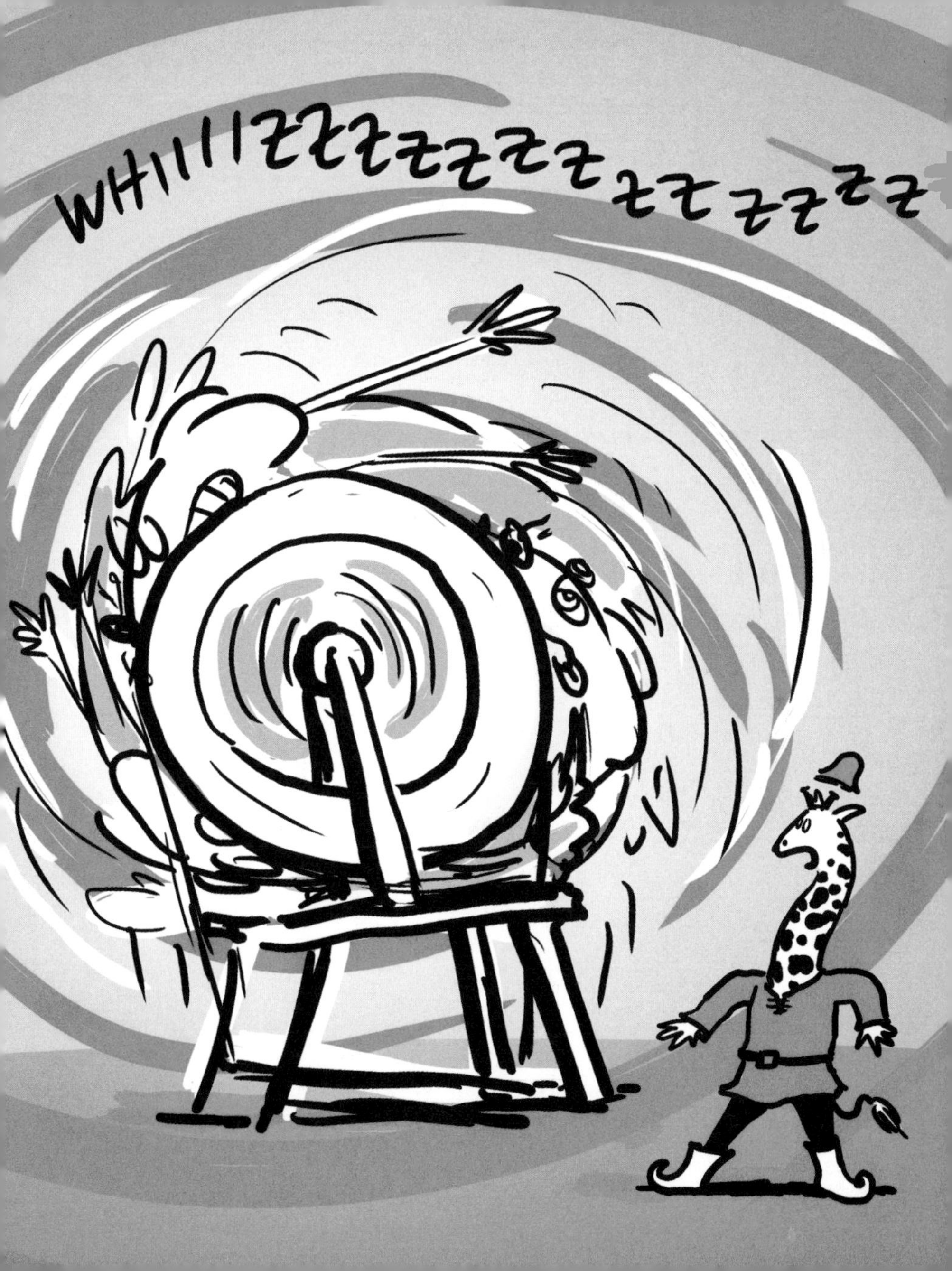
WHIIIIZZZZZZZZZZZZZZZ

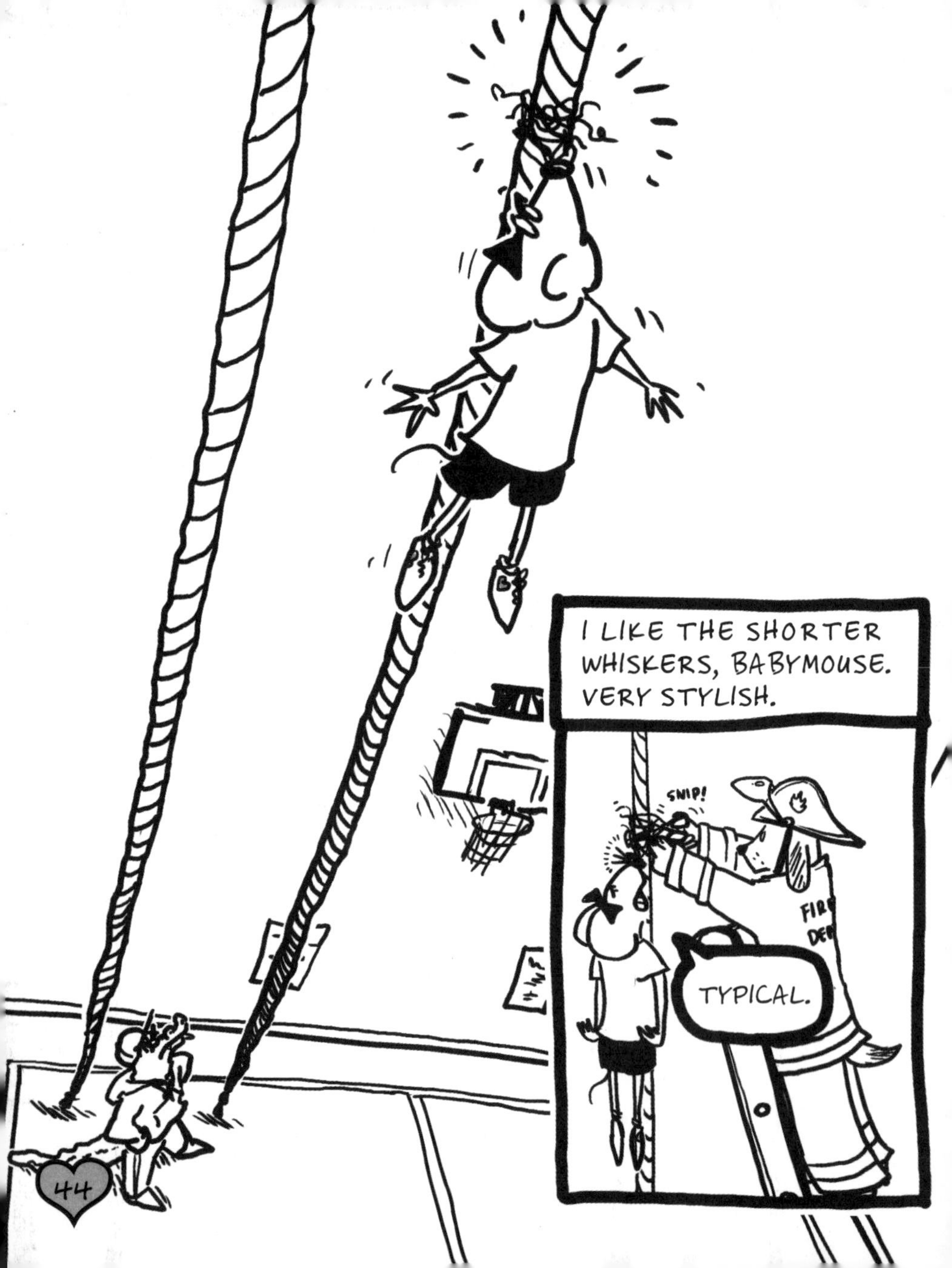
I LIKE THE SHORTER WHISKERS, BABYMOUSE. VERY STYLISH.
SNIP!
TYPICAL.

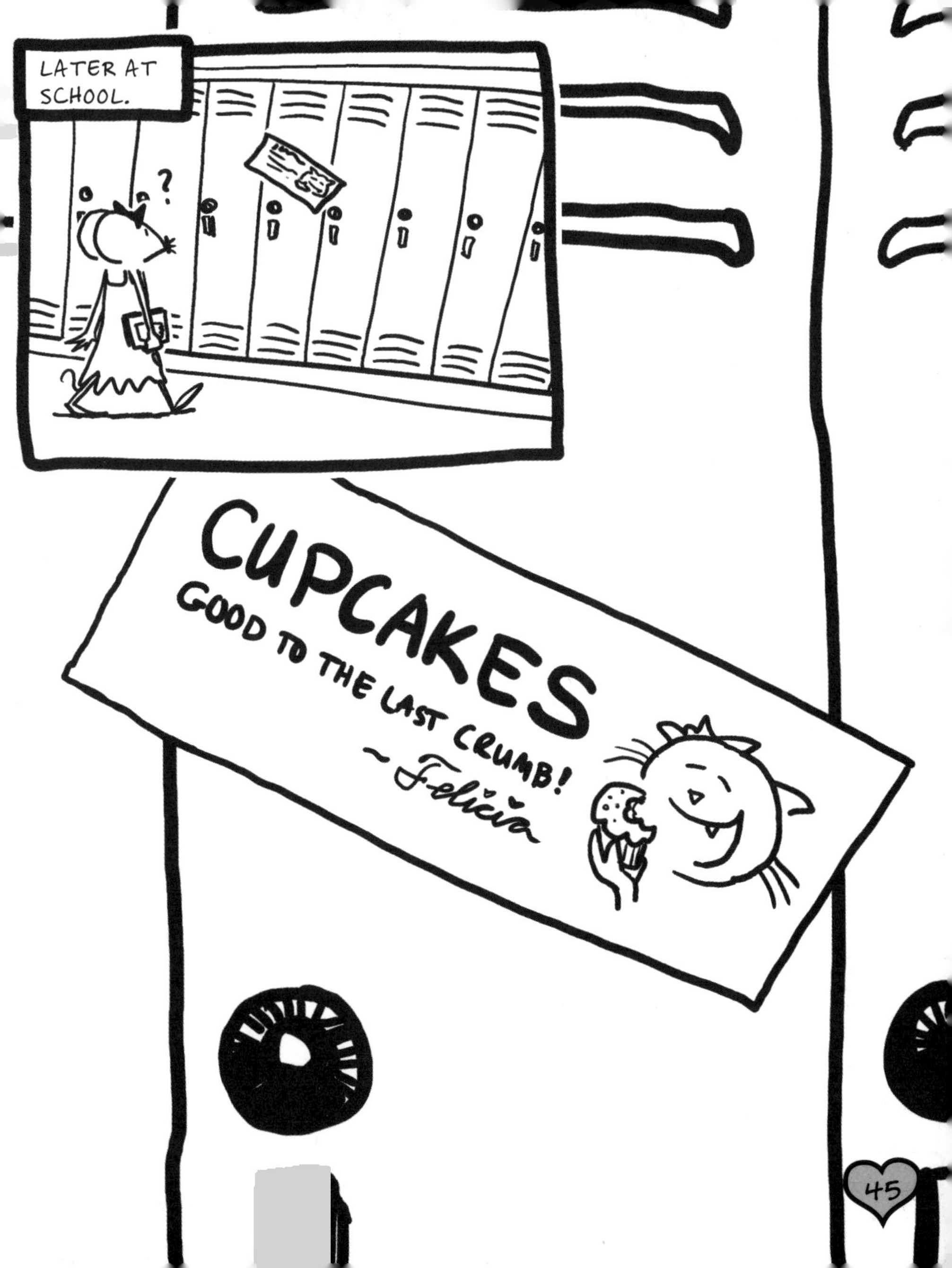

LATER AT SCHOOL.
CUPCAKES
GOOD TO THE LAST CRUMB!
~ Felicia

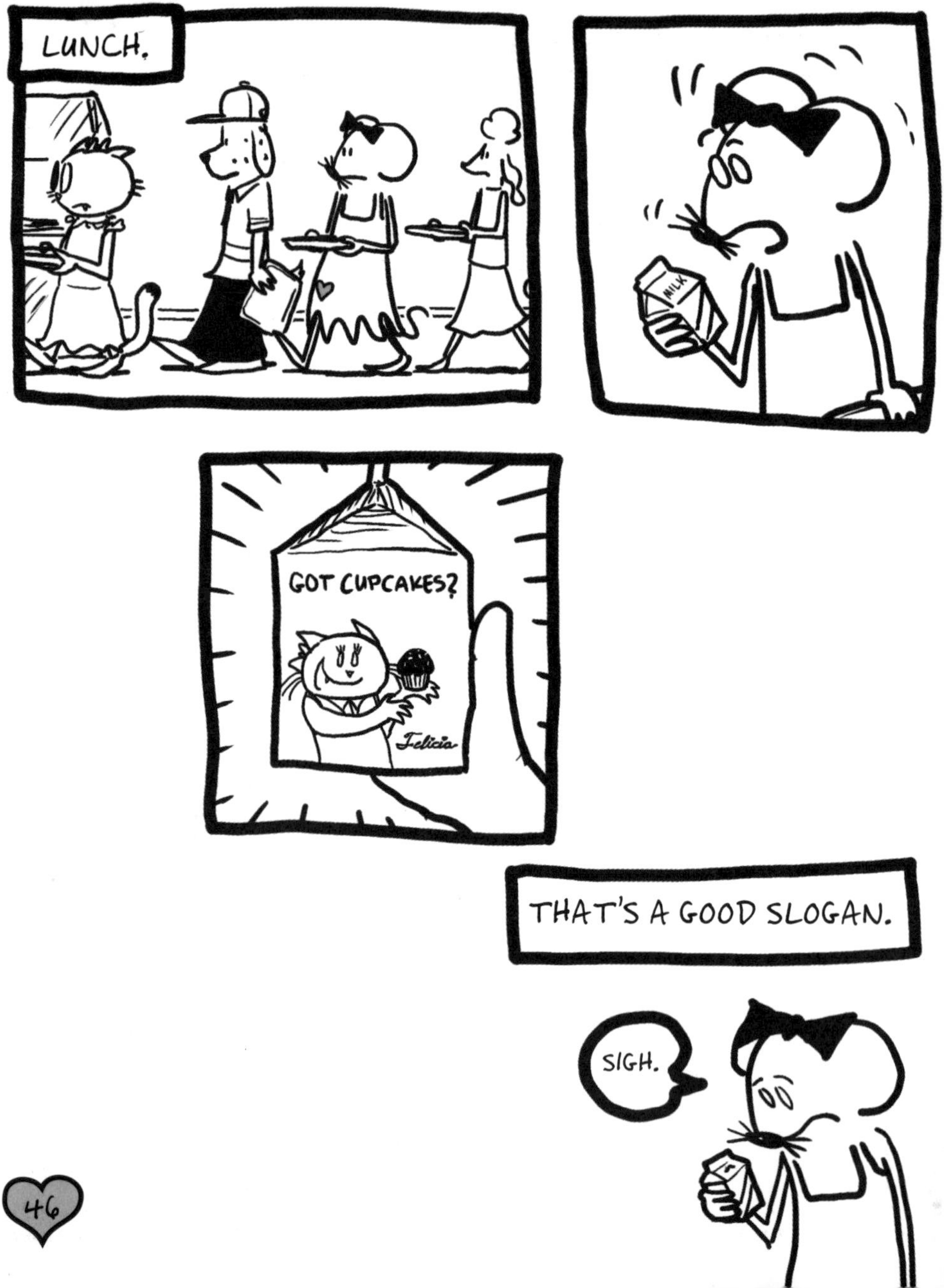
LUNCH.
MILK
GOT CUPCAKES?
Felicia
THAT'S A GOOD SLOGAN.
SIGH.

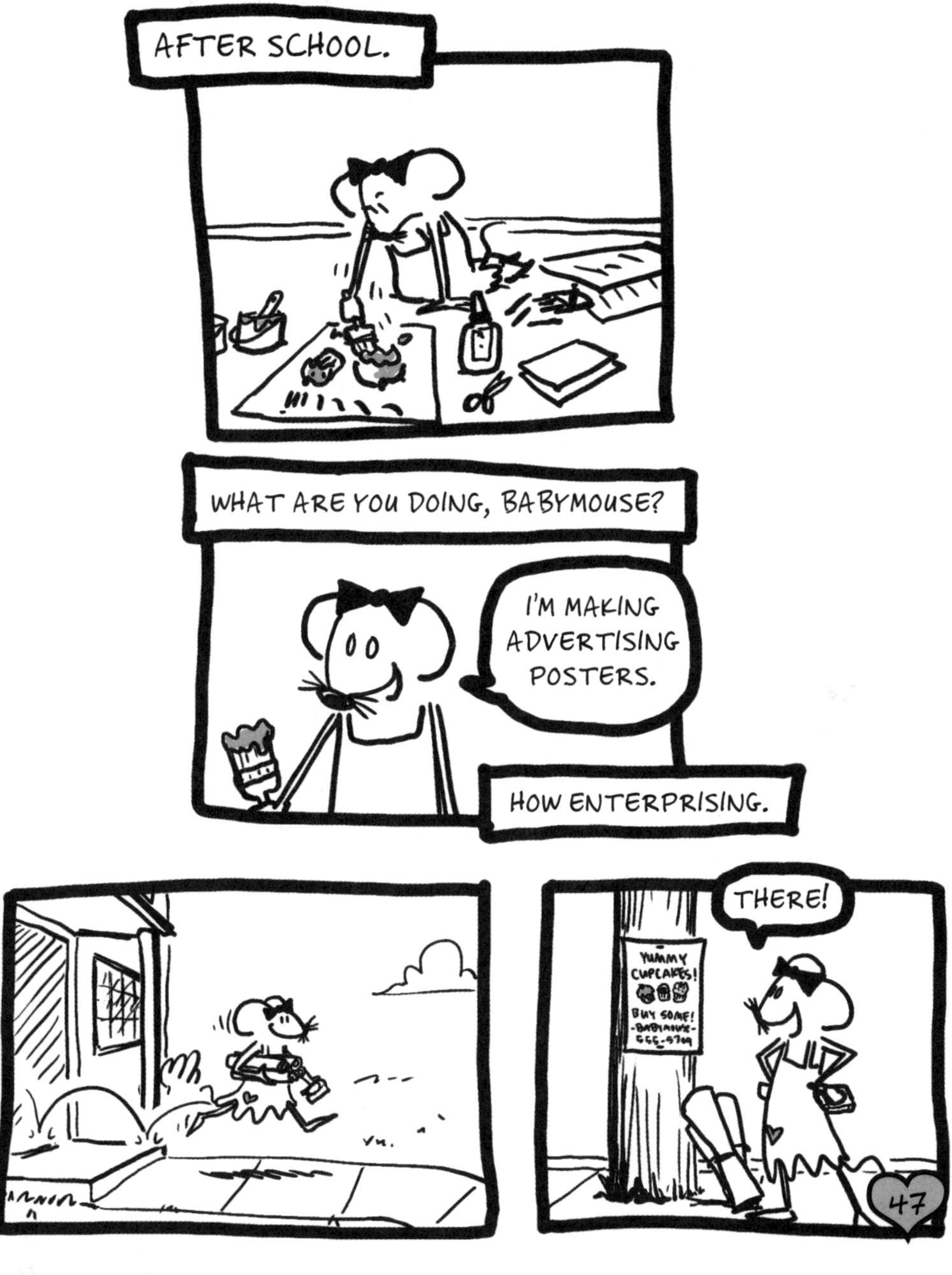
AFTER SCHOOL.
WHAT ARE YOU DOING, BABYMOUSE?
I'M MAKING ADVERTISING POSTERS.
HOW ENTERPRISING.
THERE!
YUMMY CUPCAKES!
BUY SOME!
-BABYMOUSE-
555-9709

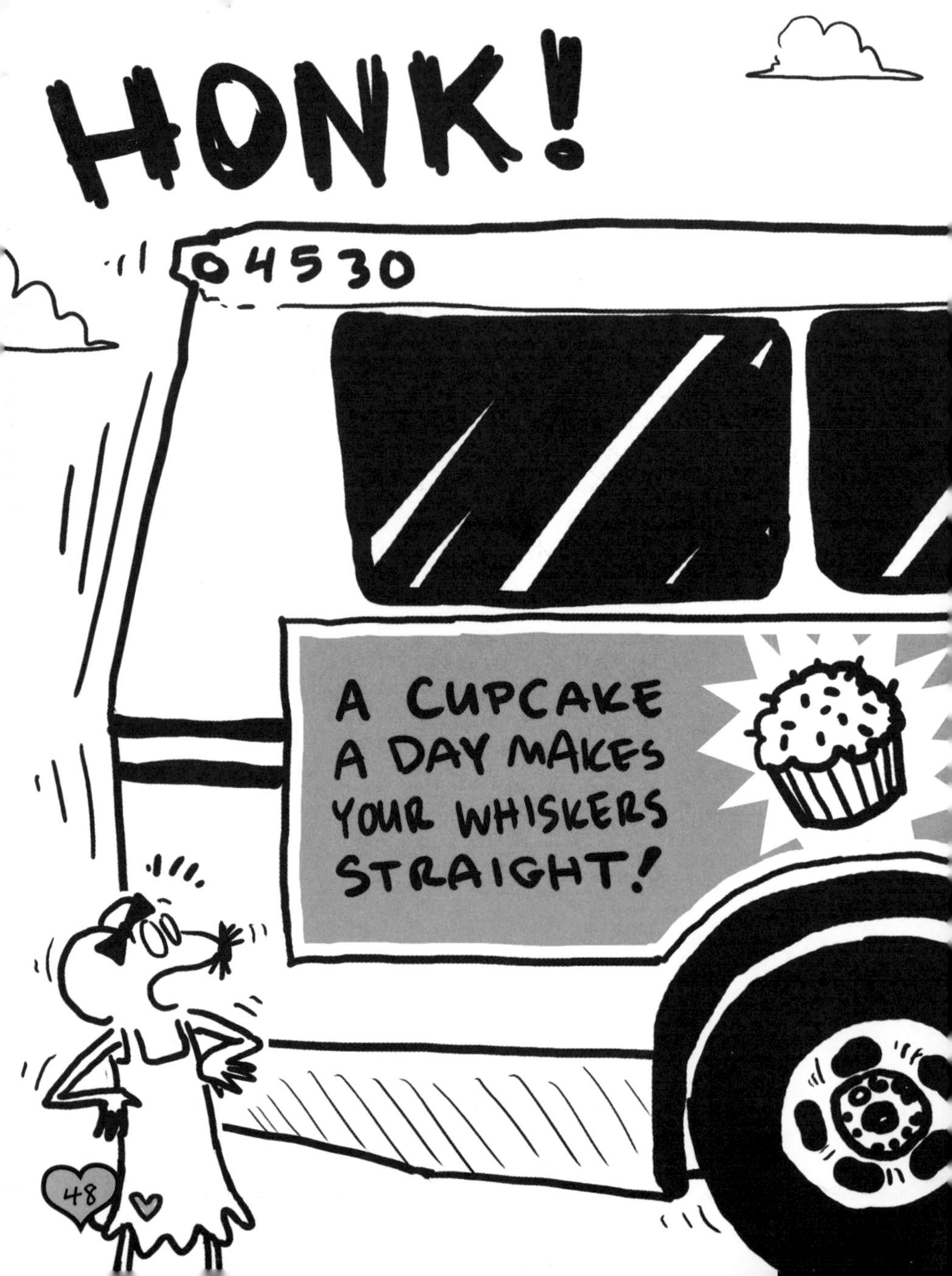
HONK!
04530
A CUPCAKE A DAY MAKES YOUR WHISKERS STRAIGHT!

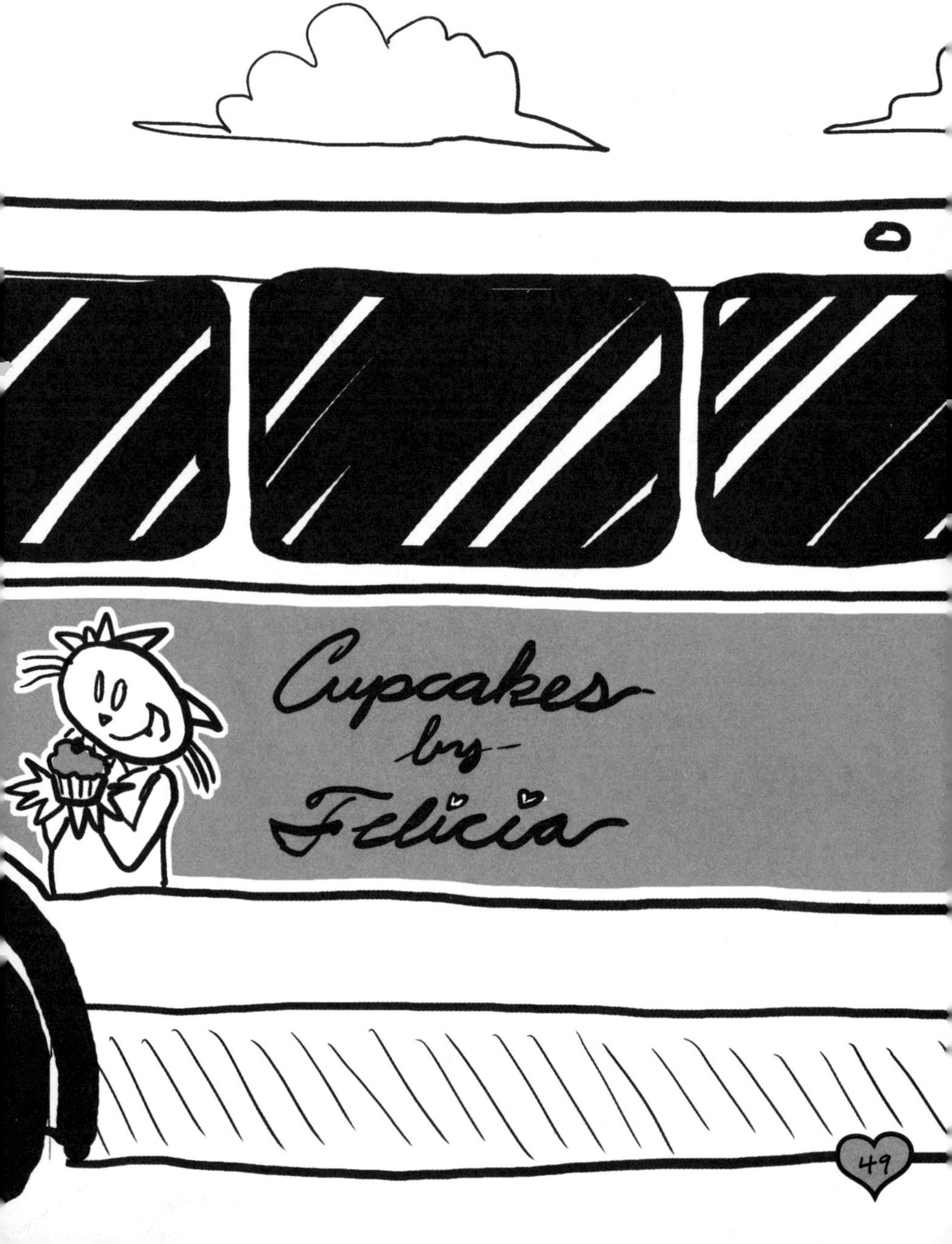
Cupcakes by Felicia

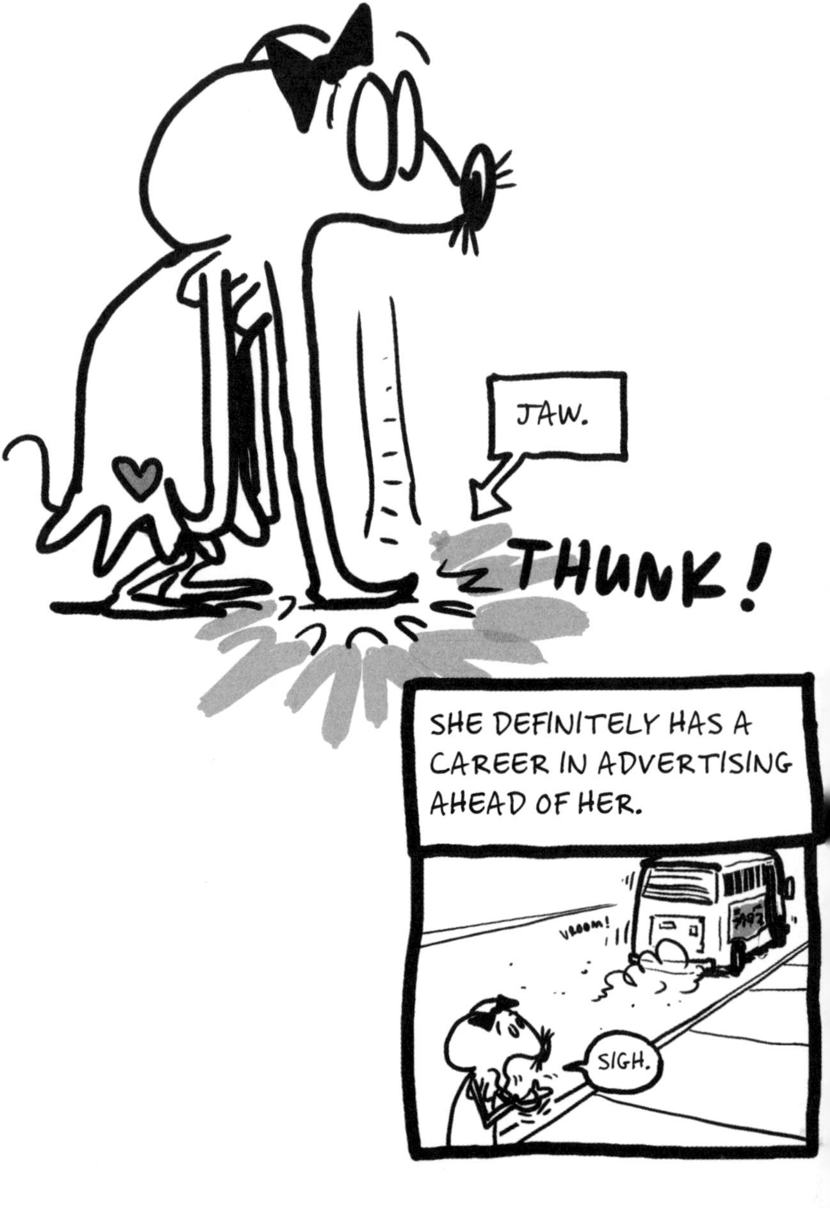
JAW.
THUNK!
SHE DEFINITELY HAS A CAREER IN ADVERTISING AHEAD OF HER.
VROOM!
SIGH.

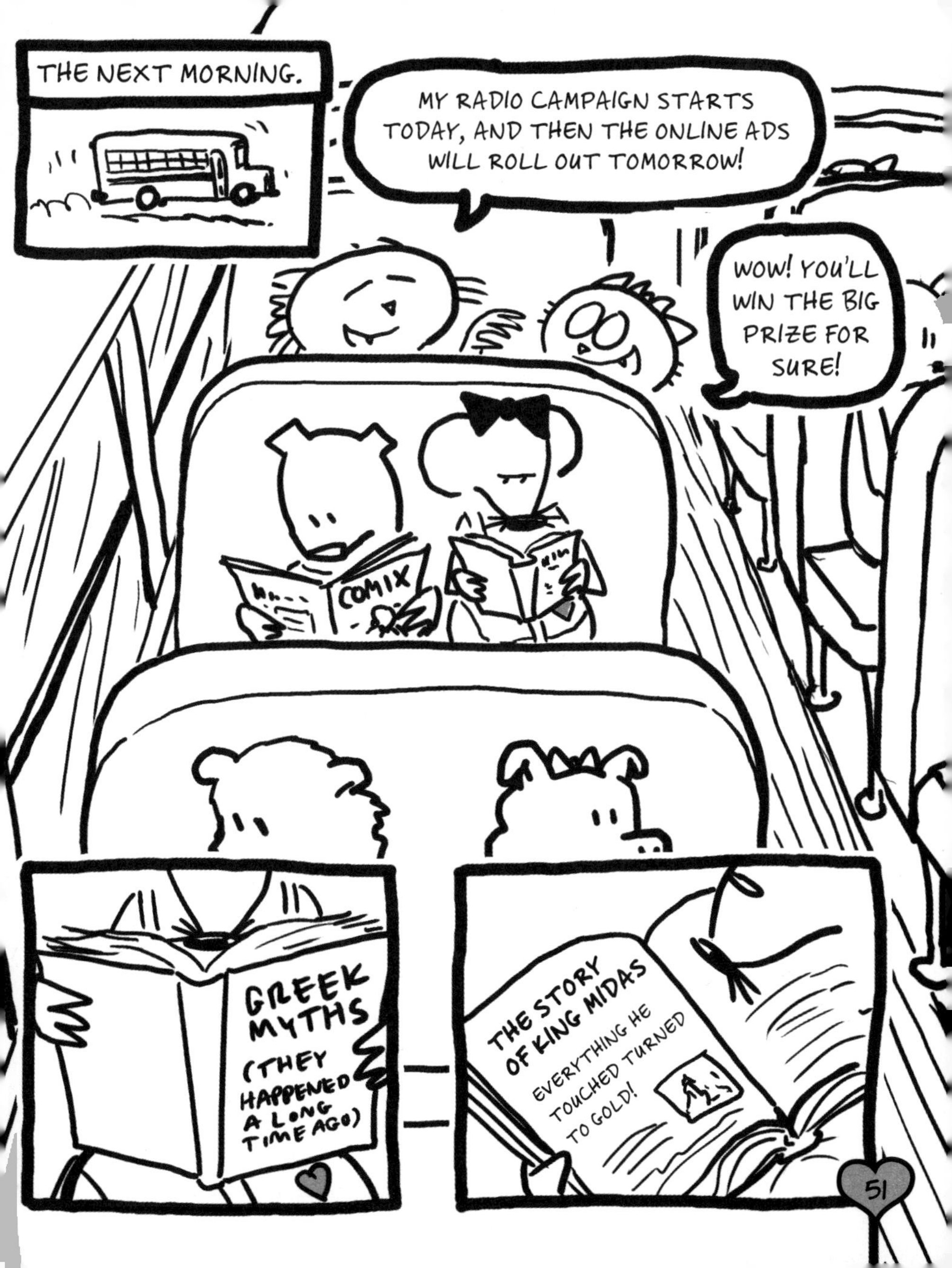
THE NEXT MORNING.
MY RADIO CAMPAIGN STARTS TODAY, AND THEN THE ONLINE ADS WILL ROLL OUT TOMORROW!
WOW! YOU'LL WIN THE BIG PRIZE FOR SURE!
COMIX
GREEK MYTHS (THEY HAPPENED A LONG TIME AGO)
THE STORY OF KING MIDAS
EVERYTHING HE TOUCHED TURNED TO GOLD!

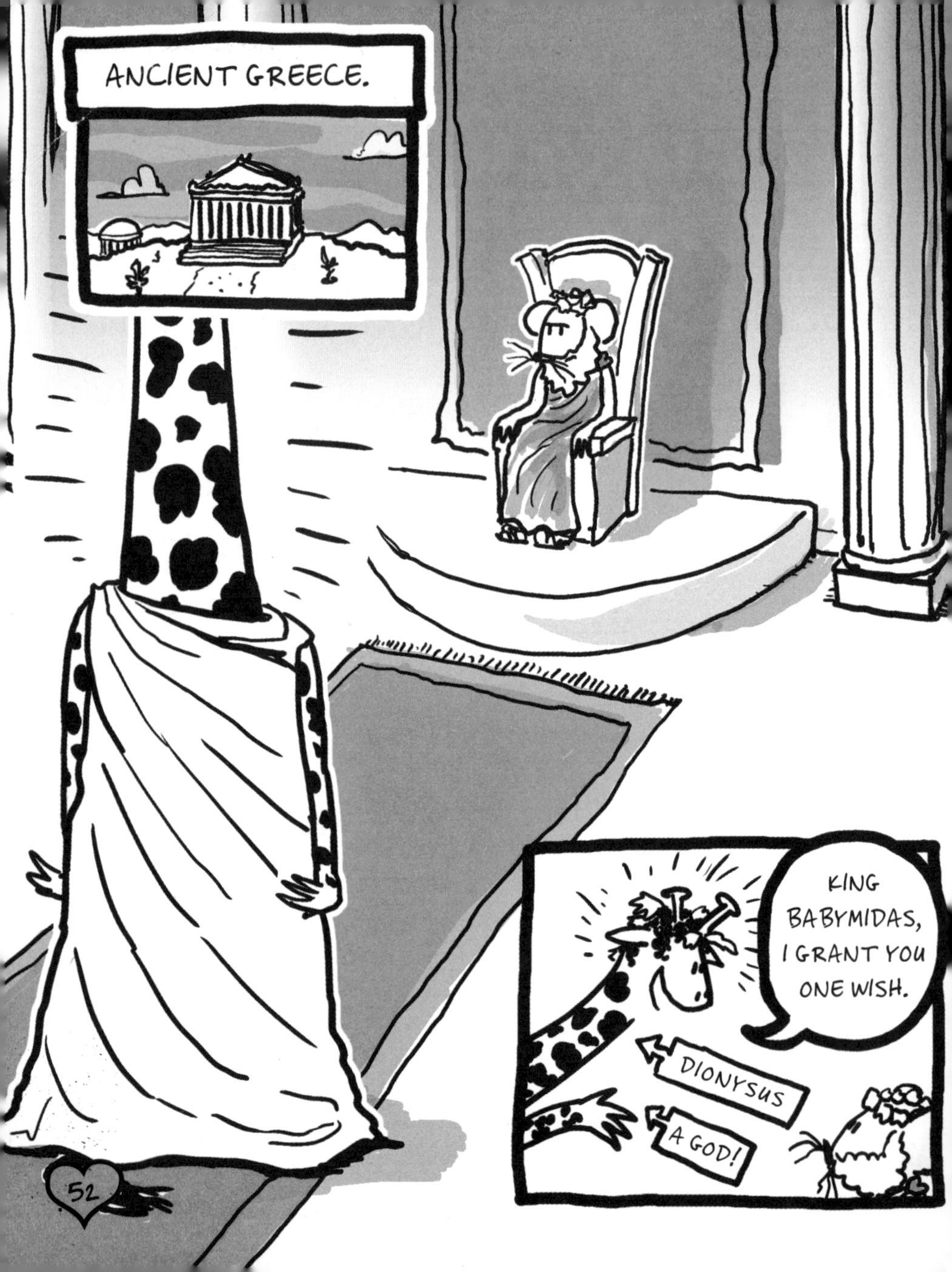
ANCIENT GREECE.
KING BABYMIDAS, I GRANT YOU ONE WISH.
DIONYSUS
A GOD!

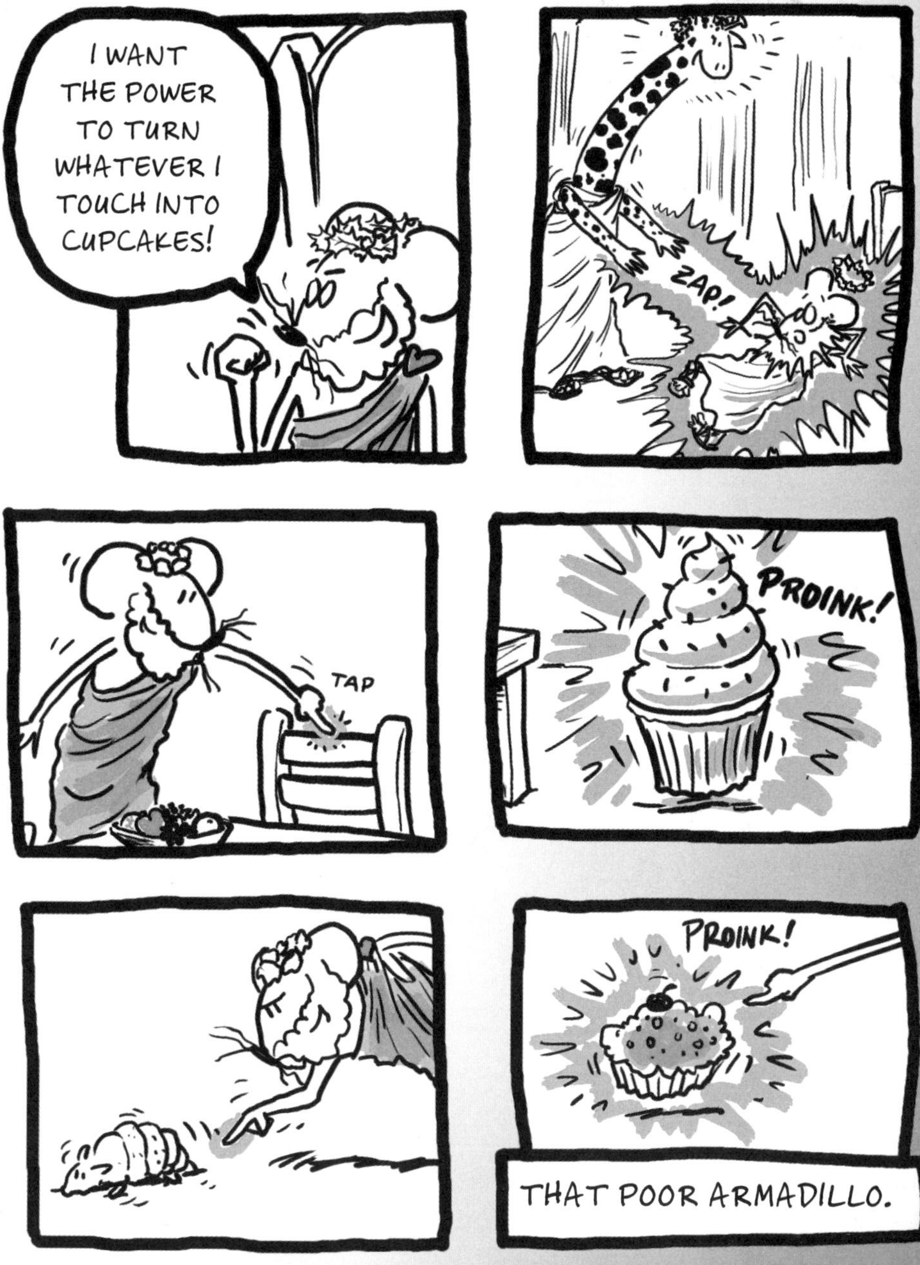
I WANT THE POWER TO TURN WHATEVER I TOUCH INTO CUPCAKES!
ZAP!
TAP
PROINK!
PROINK!
THAT POOR ARMADILLO.

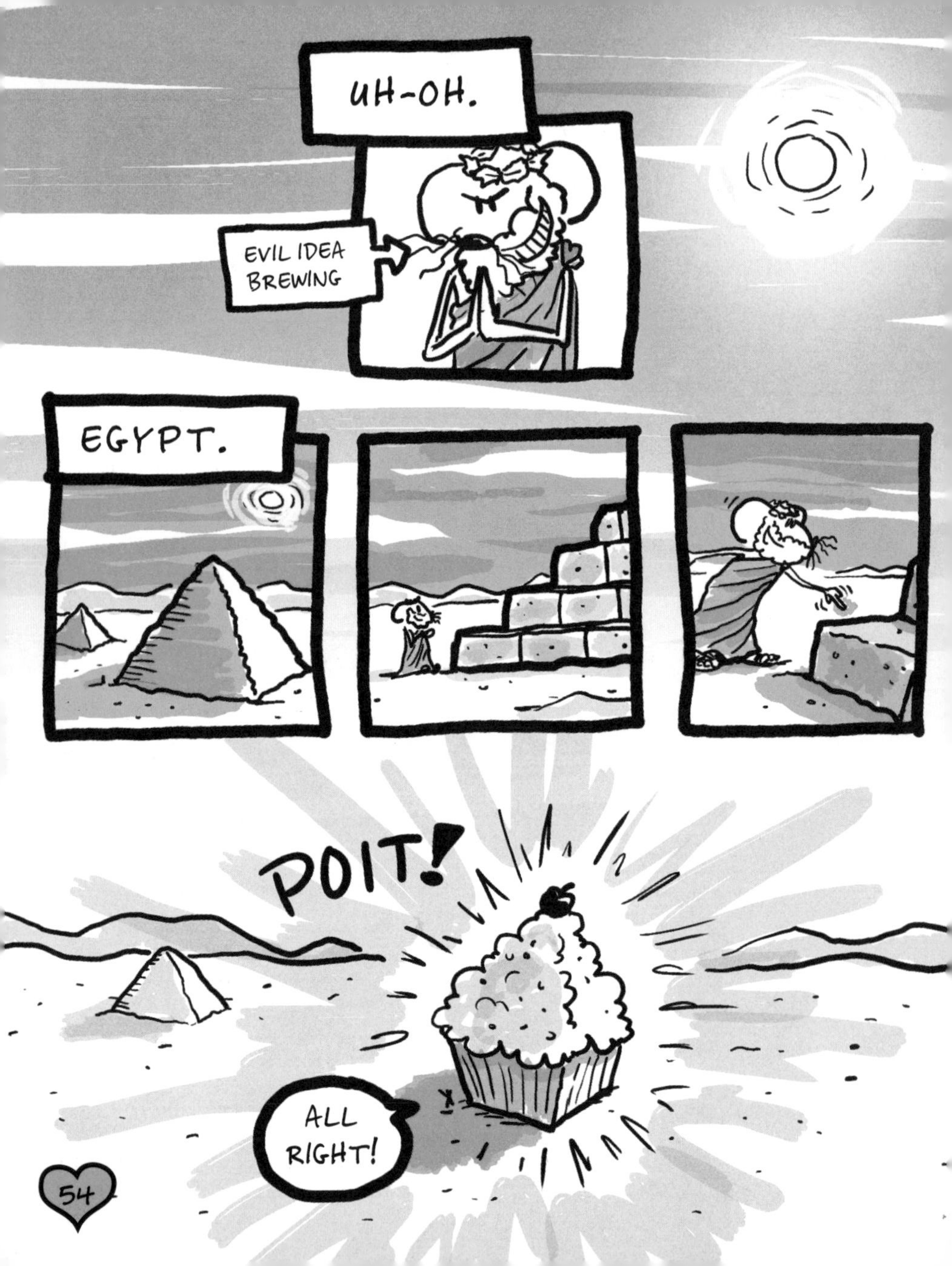
UH-OH.
EVIL IDEA BREWING
EGYPT.
POIT!
ALL RIGHT!

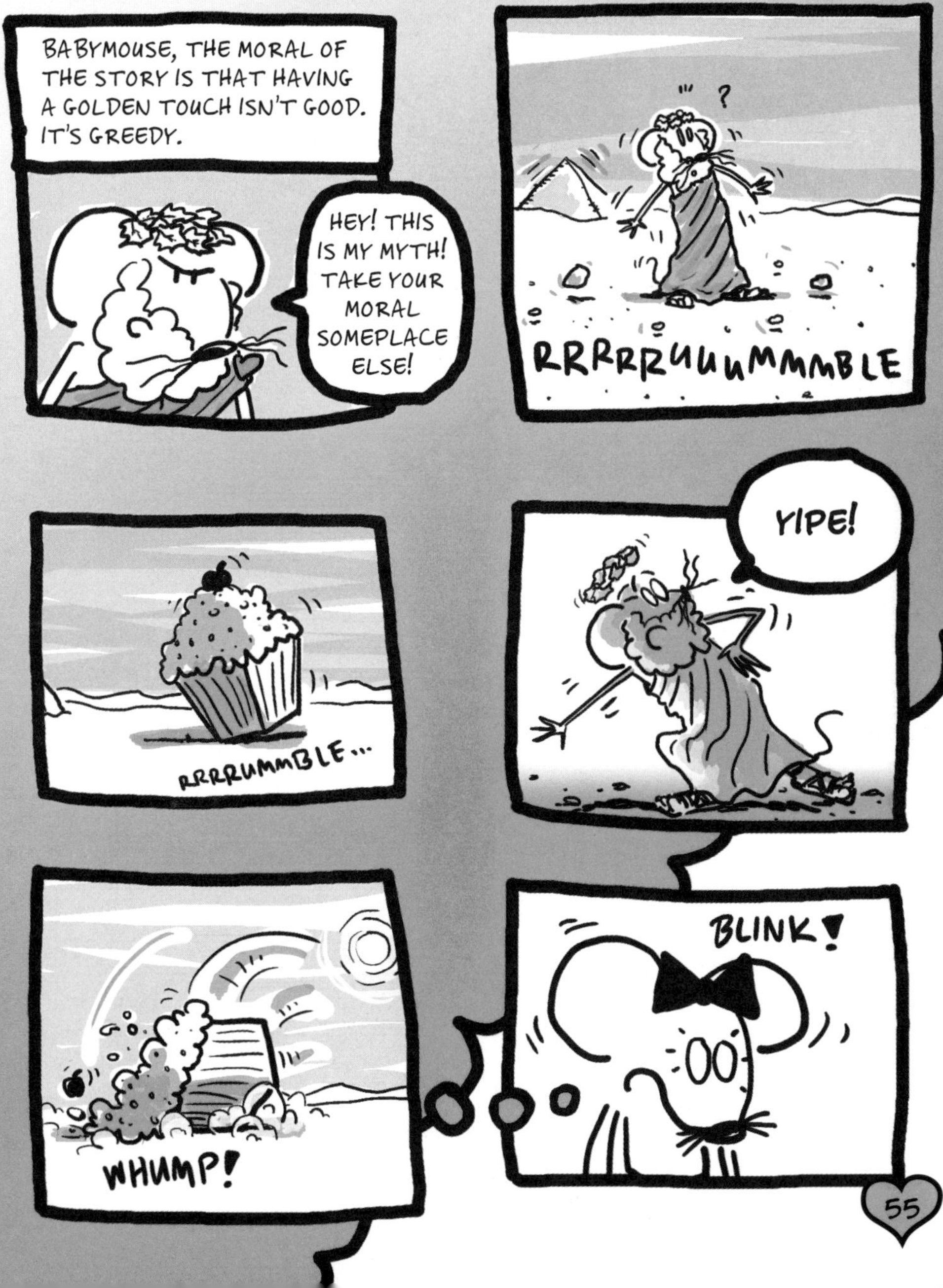

BABYMOUSE, THE MORAL OF THE STORY IS THAT HAVING A GOLDEN TOUCH ISN'T GOOD. IT'S GREEDY.
HEY! THIS IS MY MYTH! TAKE YOUR MORAL SOMEPLACE ELSE!
RRRRRUUUMMMBLE
RRRRUMMBLE...
YIPE!
WHUMP!
BLINK!

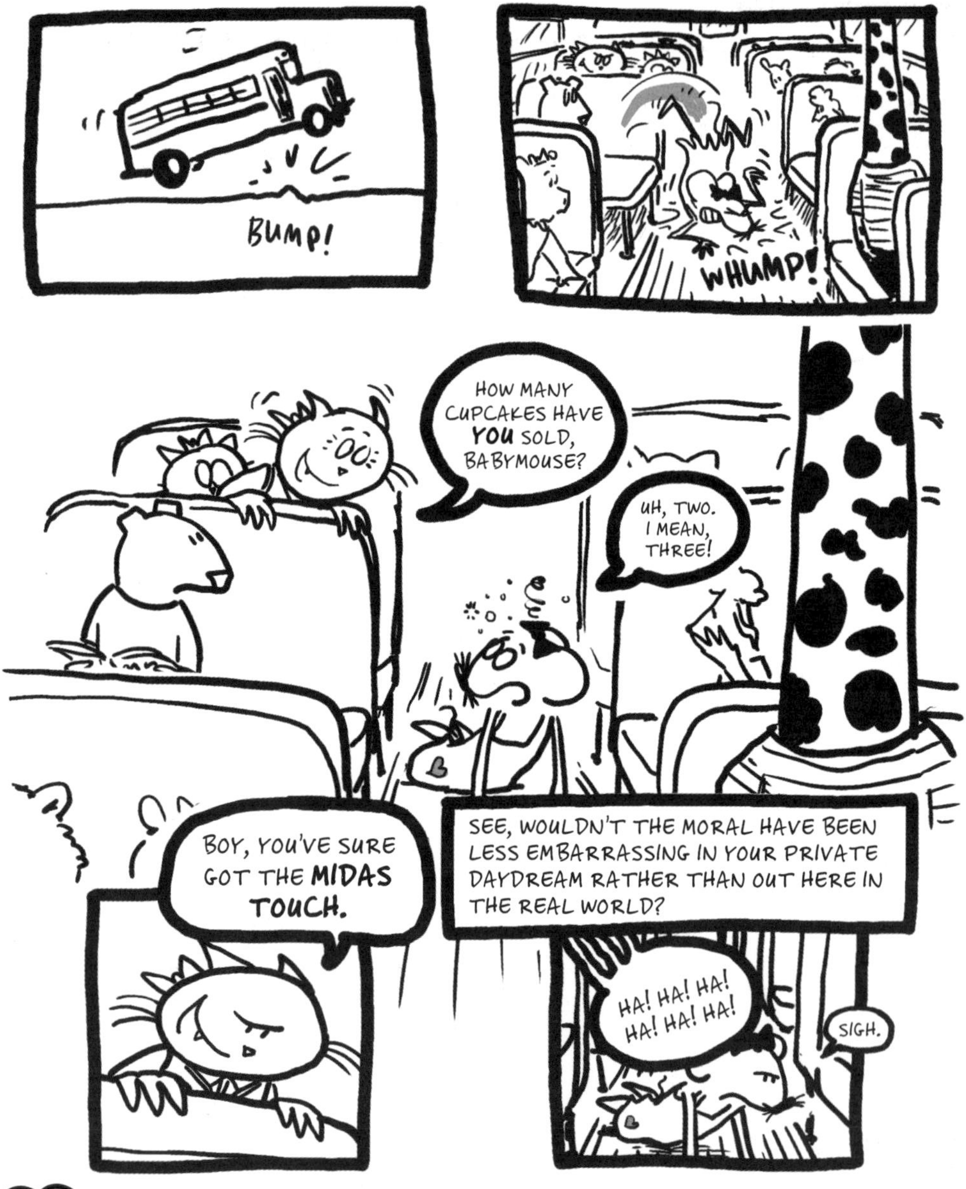
BUMP!
WHUMP!
HOW MANY CUPCAKES HAVE **YOU** SOLD, BABYMOUSE?
UH, TWO. I MEAN, THREE!
BOY, YOU'VE SURE GOT THE **MIDAS TOUCH.**
SEE, WOULDN'T THE MORAL HAVE BEEN LESS EMBARRASSING IN YOUR PRIVATE DAYDREAM RATHER THAN OUT HERE IN THE REAL WORLD?
HA! HA! HA! HA! HA! HA!
SIGH.

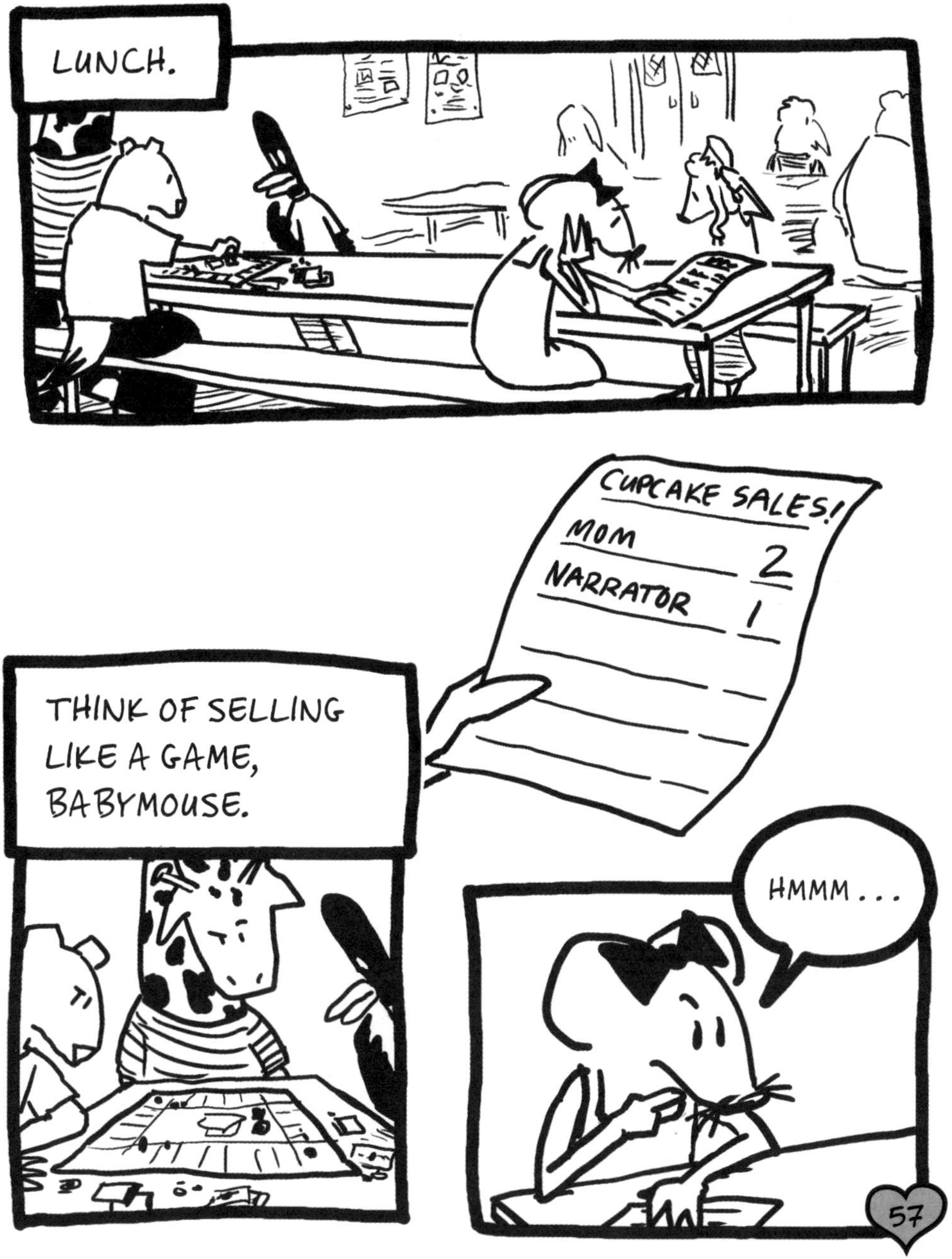
LUNCH.
CUPCAKE SALES!
MOM 2
NARRATOR 1
THINK OF SELLING LIKE A GAME, BABYMOUSE.
HMMM...

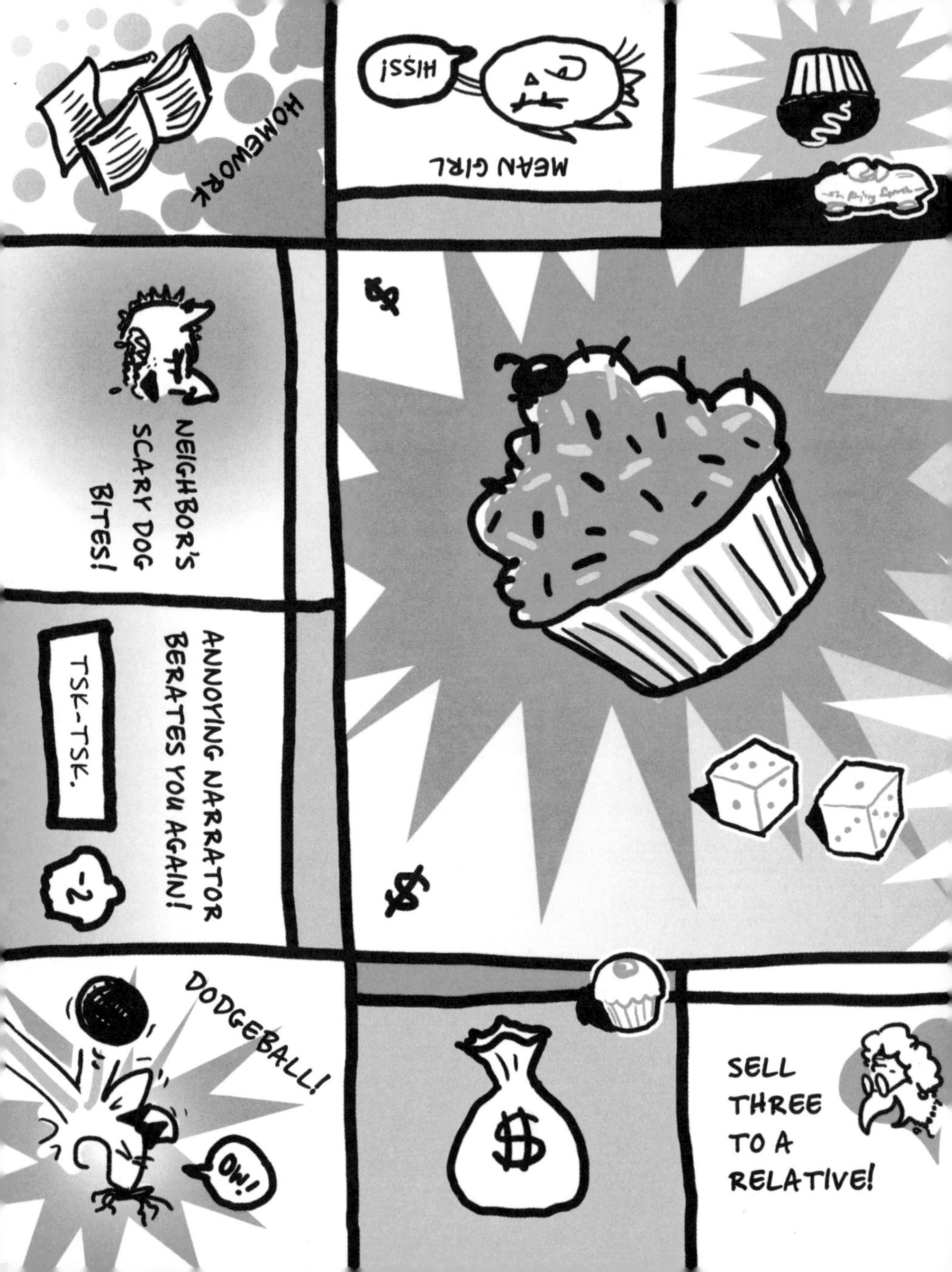
HOMEWORK
MEAN GIRL
HISS!
NEIGHBOR'S SCARY DOG BITES!
ANNOYING NARRATOR BERATES YOU AGAIN!
TSK-TSK.
-2
DODGEBALL!
OW!
SELL THREE TO A RELATIVE!

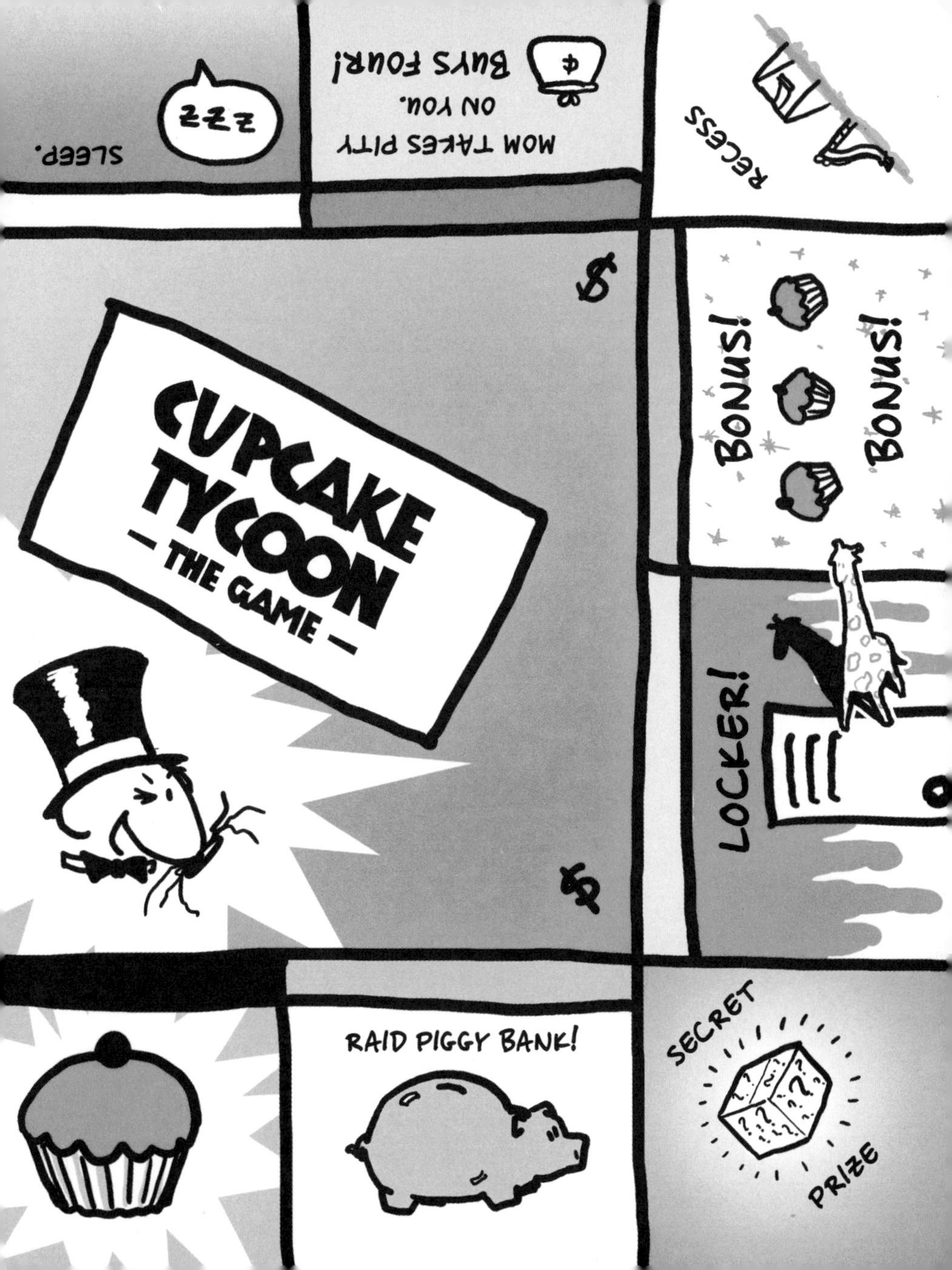
SLEEP.
ZZZ
MOM TAKES PITY ON YOU. BUYS FOUR!
RECESS
BONUS!
BONUS!
CUPCAKE TYCOON
— THE GAME —
LOCKER!
RAID PIGGY BANK!
SECRET PRIZE

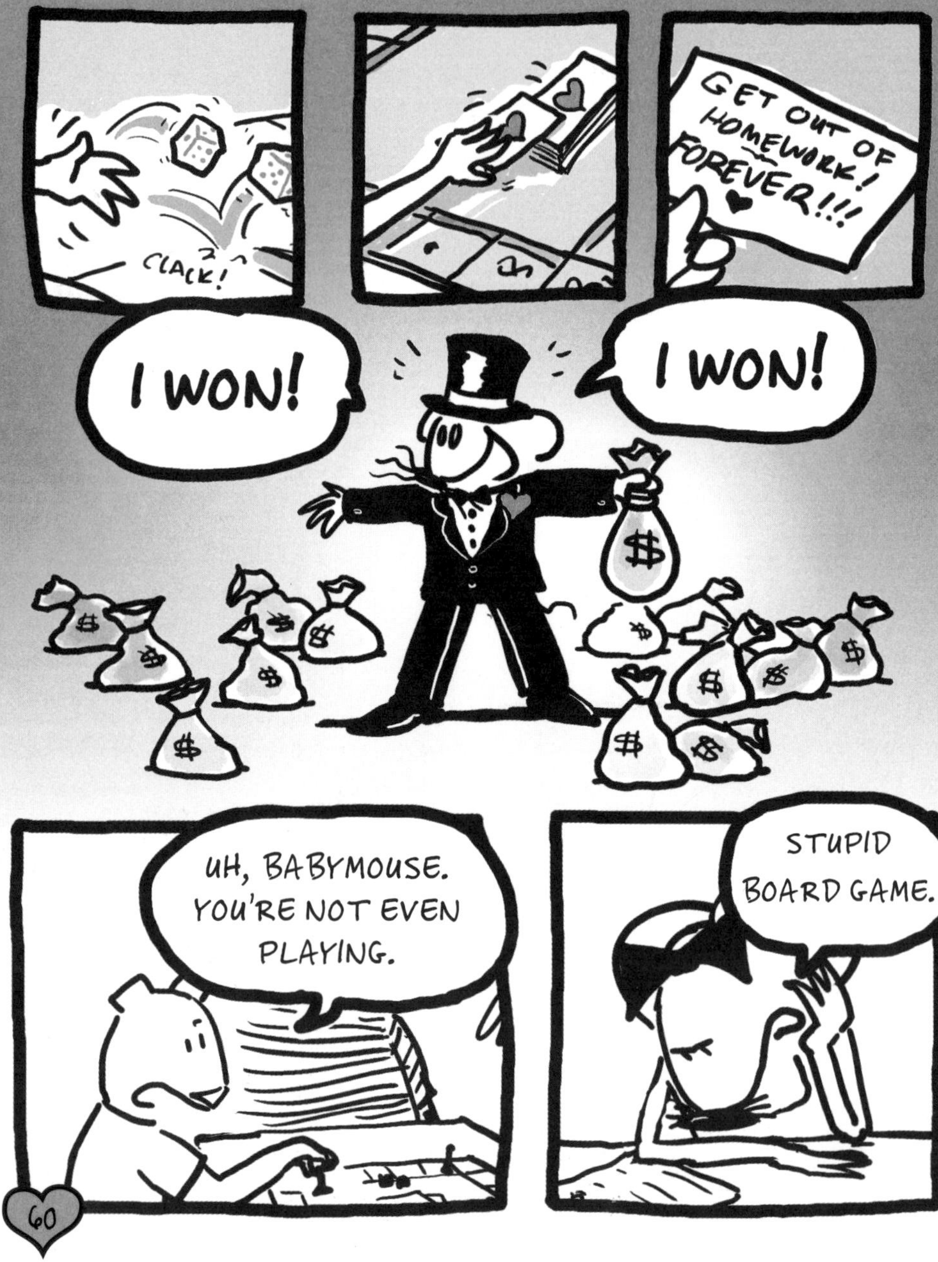
CLACK!
GET OUT OF HOMEWORK! FOREVER!!!
I WON!
I WON!
UH, BABYMOUSE. YOU'RE NOT EVEN PLAYING.
STUPID BOARD GAME.

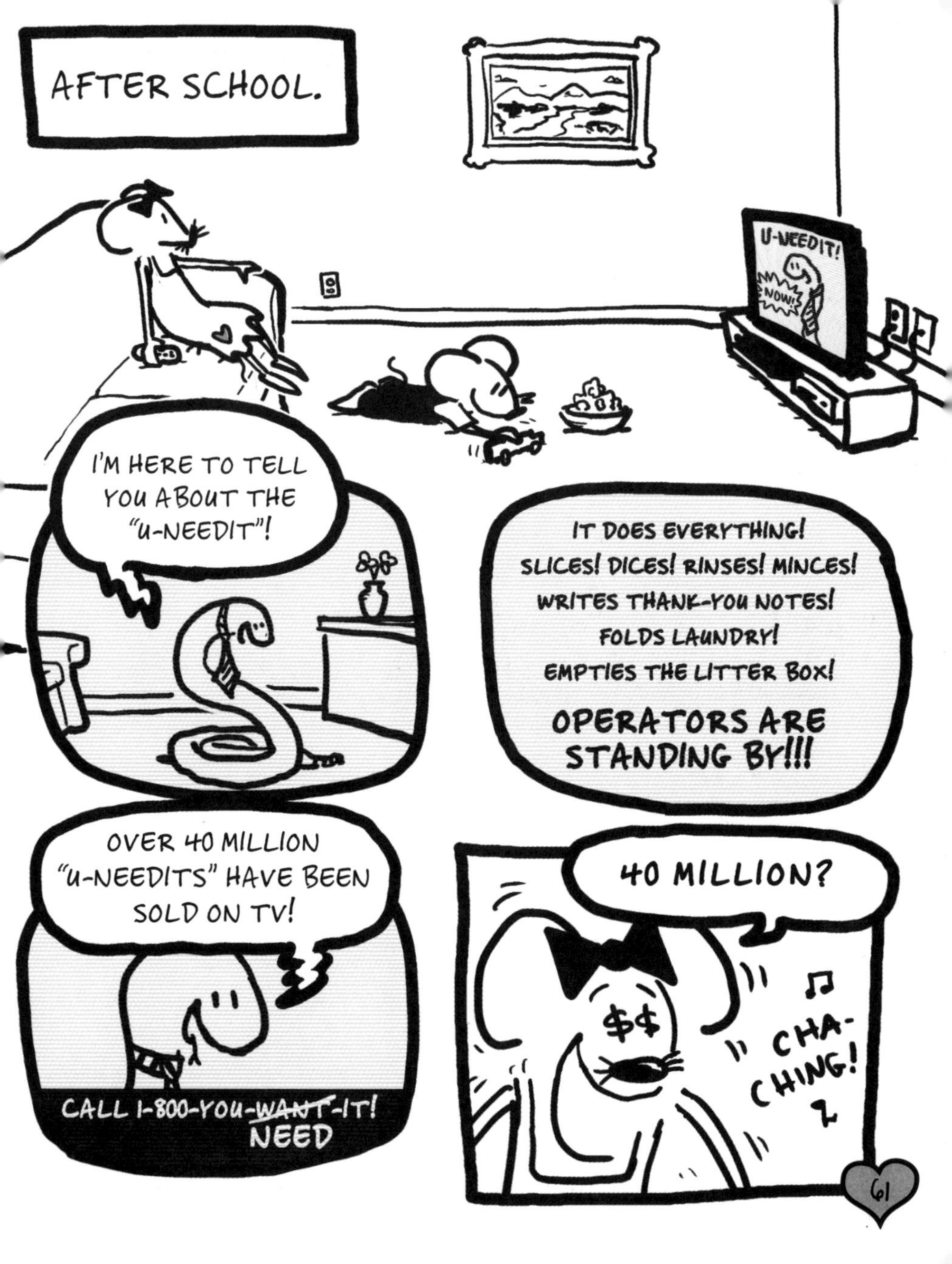

AFTER SCHOOL.
U-NEEDIT!
NOW!
I'M HERE TO TELL YOU ABOUT THE "U-NEEDIT"!
IT DOES EVERYTHING! SLICES! DICES! RINSES! MINCES! WRITES THANK-YOU NOTES! FOLDS LAUNDRY! EMPTIES THE LITTER BOX!
OPERATORS ARE STANDING BY!!!
OVER 40 MILLION "U-NEEDITS" HAVE BEEN SOLD ON TV!
CALL 1-800-YOU-WANT-IT! NEED
40 MILLION?
CHA-CHING!

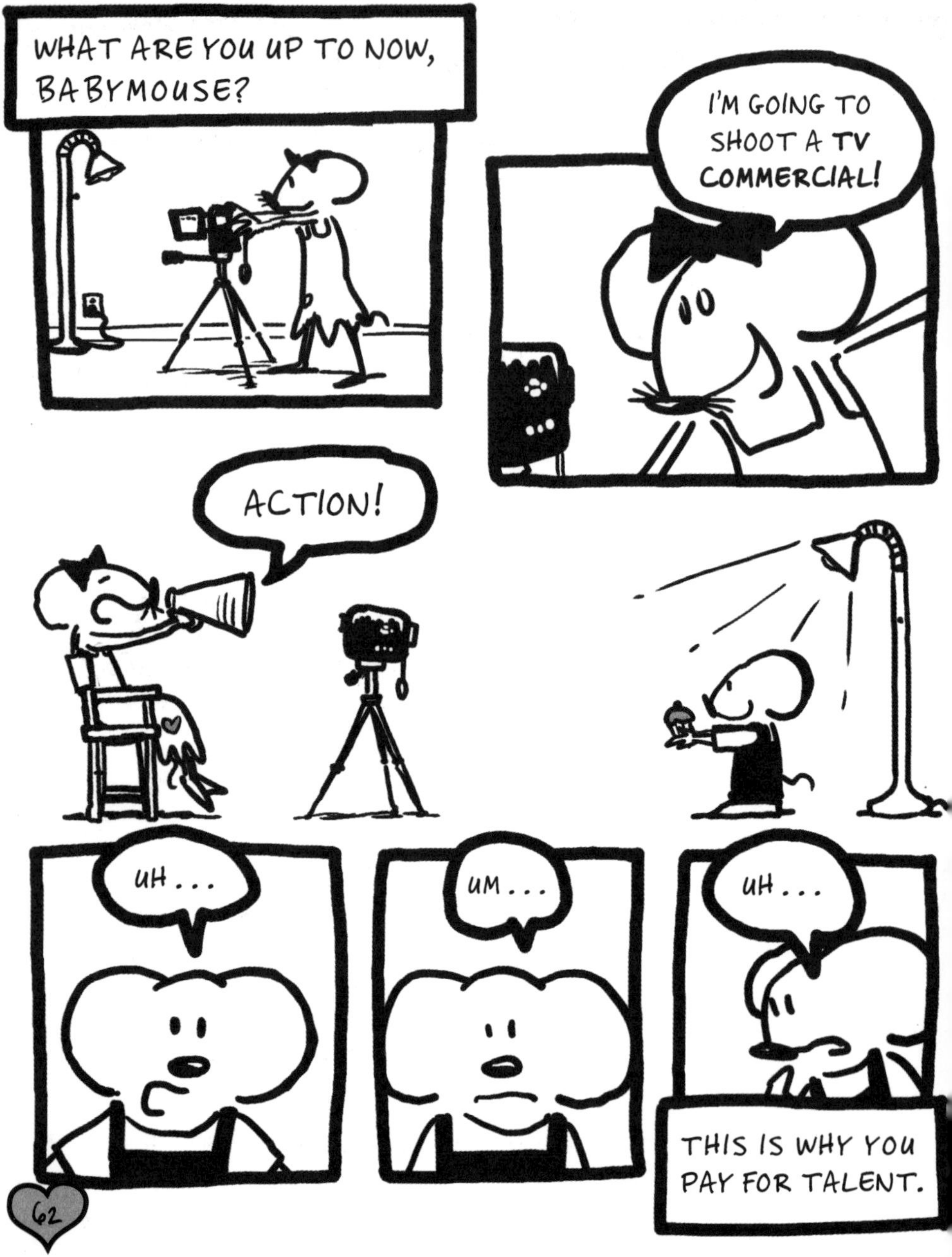
WHAT ARE YOU UP TO NOW, BABYMOUSE?
I'M GOING TO SHOOT A **TV COMMERCIAL!**
ACTION!
UH . . .
UM . . .
UH . . .
THIS IS WHY YOU PAY FOR TALENT.

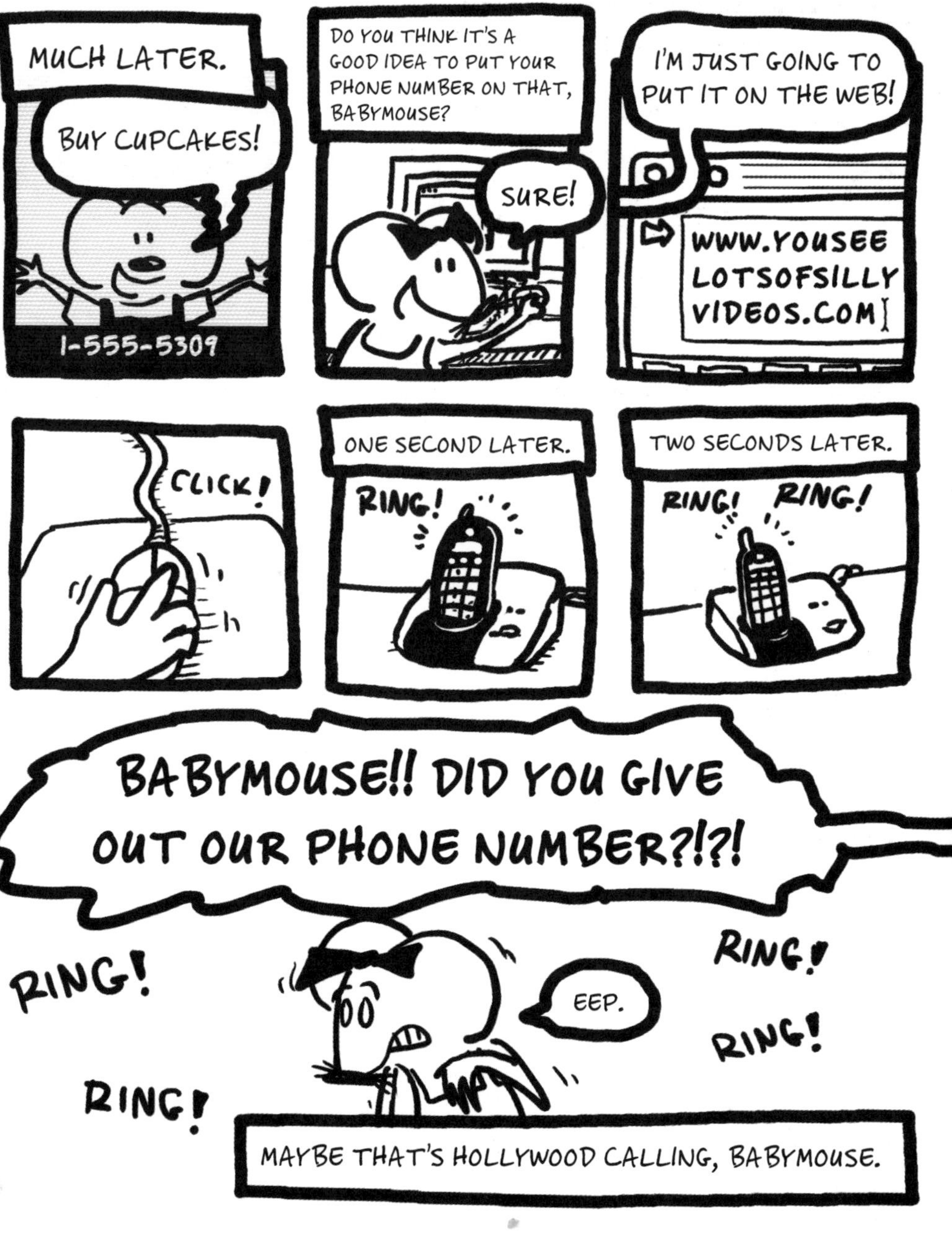
MUCH LATER.
BUY CUPCAKES!
1-555-5309
DO YOU THINK IT'S A GOOD IDEA TO PUT YOUR PHONE NUMBER ON THAT, BABYMOUSE?
SURE!
I'M JUST GOING TO PUT IT ON THE WEB!
WWW.YOUSEELOTSOFSILLYVIDEOS.COM
CLICK!
ONE SECOND LATER.
RING!
TWO SECONDS LATER.
RING! RING!
BABYMOUSE!! DID YOU GIVE OUT OUR PHONE NUMBER?!?!
RING!
EEP.
RING!
RING!
RING!
MAYBE THAT'S HOLLYWOOD CALLING, BABYMOUSE.

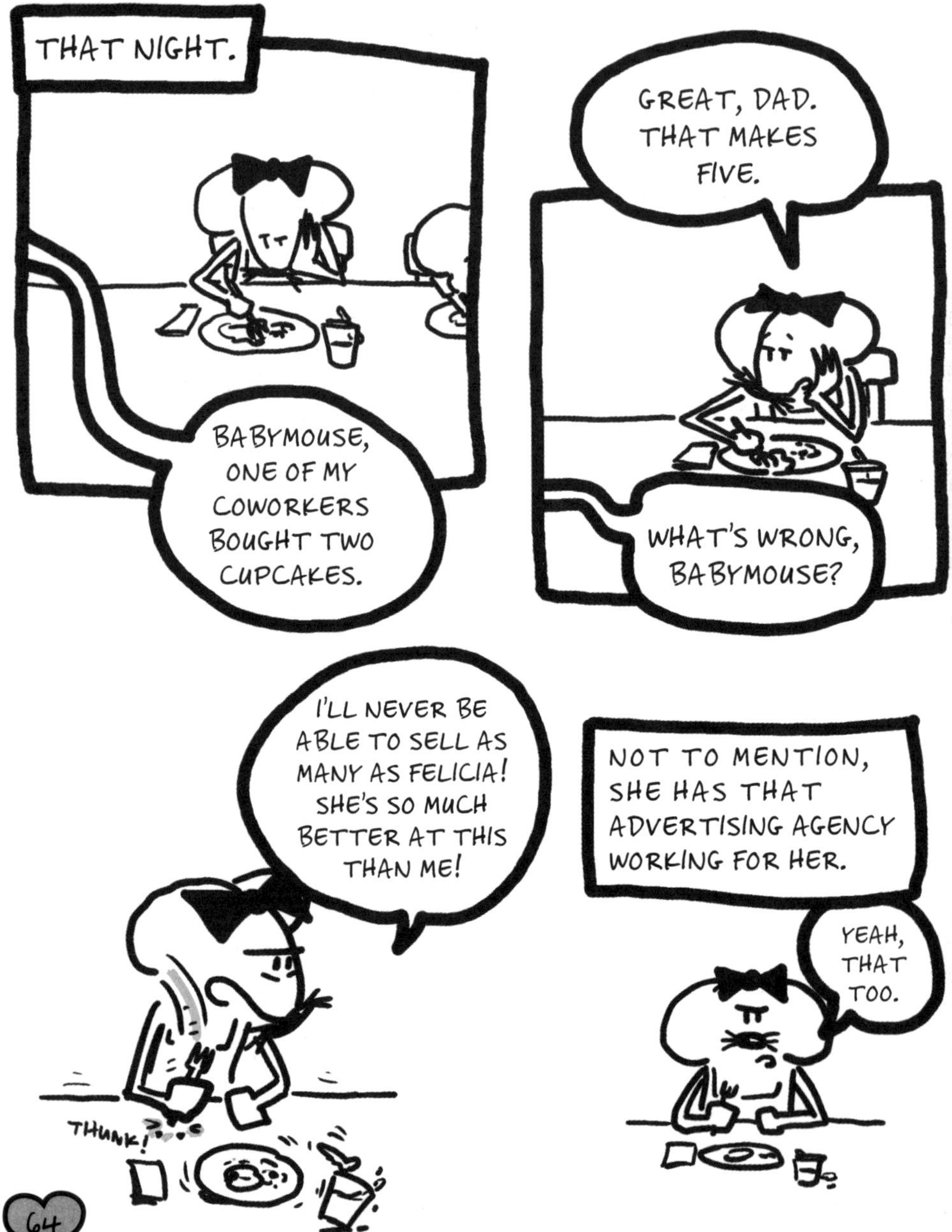
THAT NIGHT.
BABYMOUSE, ONE OF MY COWORKERS BOUGHT TWO CUPCAKES.
GREAT, DAD. THAT MAKES FIVE.
WHAT'S WRONG, BABYMOUSE?
I'LL NEVER BE ABLE TO SELL AS MANY AS FELICIA! SHE'S SO MUCH BETTER AT THIS THAN ME!
THUNK!
NOT TO MENTION, SHE HAS THAT ADVERTISING AGENCY WORKING FOR HER.
YEAH, THAT TOO.

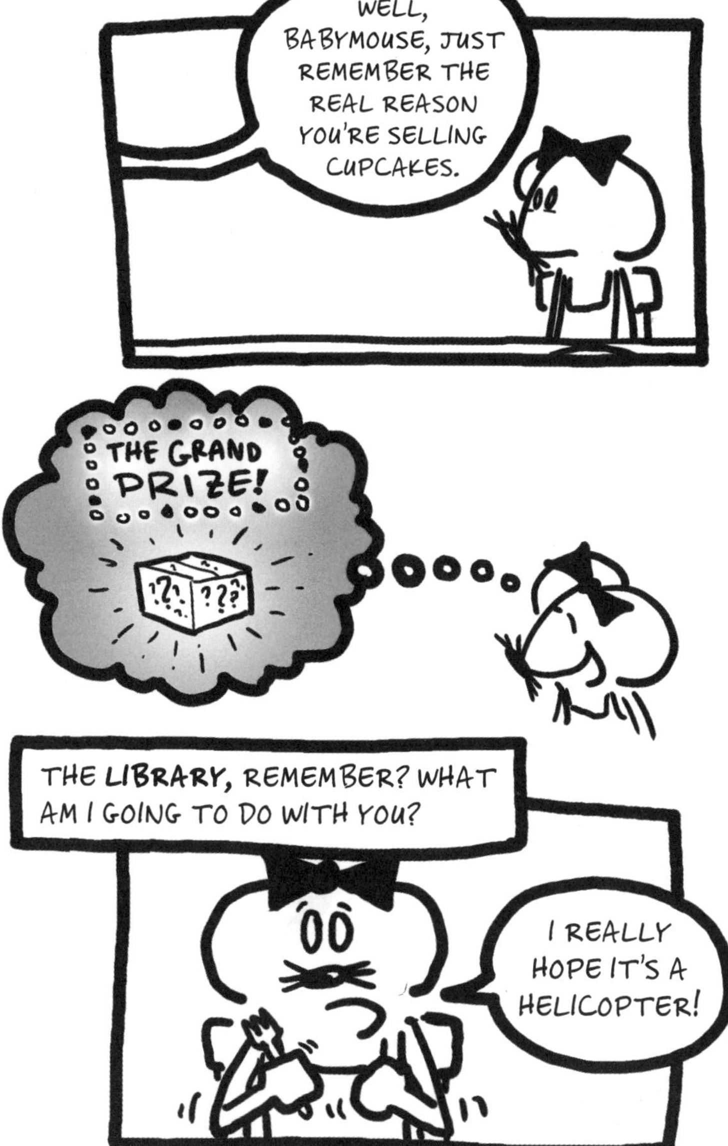
WELL, BABYMOUSE, JUST REMEMBER THE REAL REASON YOU'RE SELLING CUPCAKES.
THE GRAND PRIZE!
???
THE LIBRARY, REMEMBER? WHAT AM I GOING TO DO WITH YOU?
I REALLY HOPE IT'S A HELICOPTER!

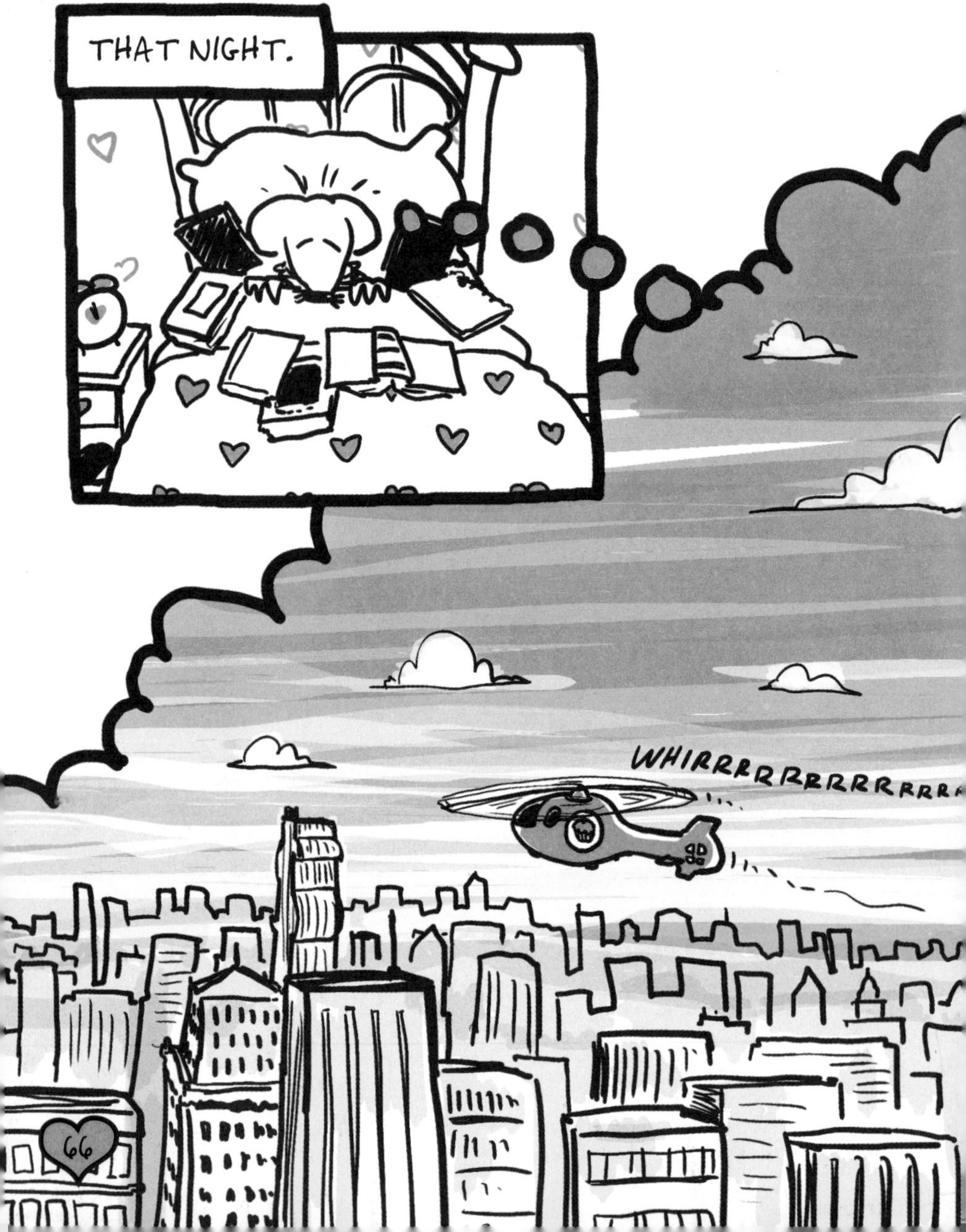
THAT NIGHT.
WHIRRRRRRRRRRRRRR

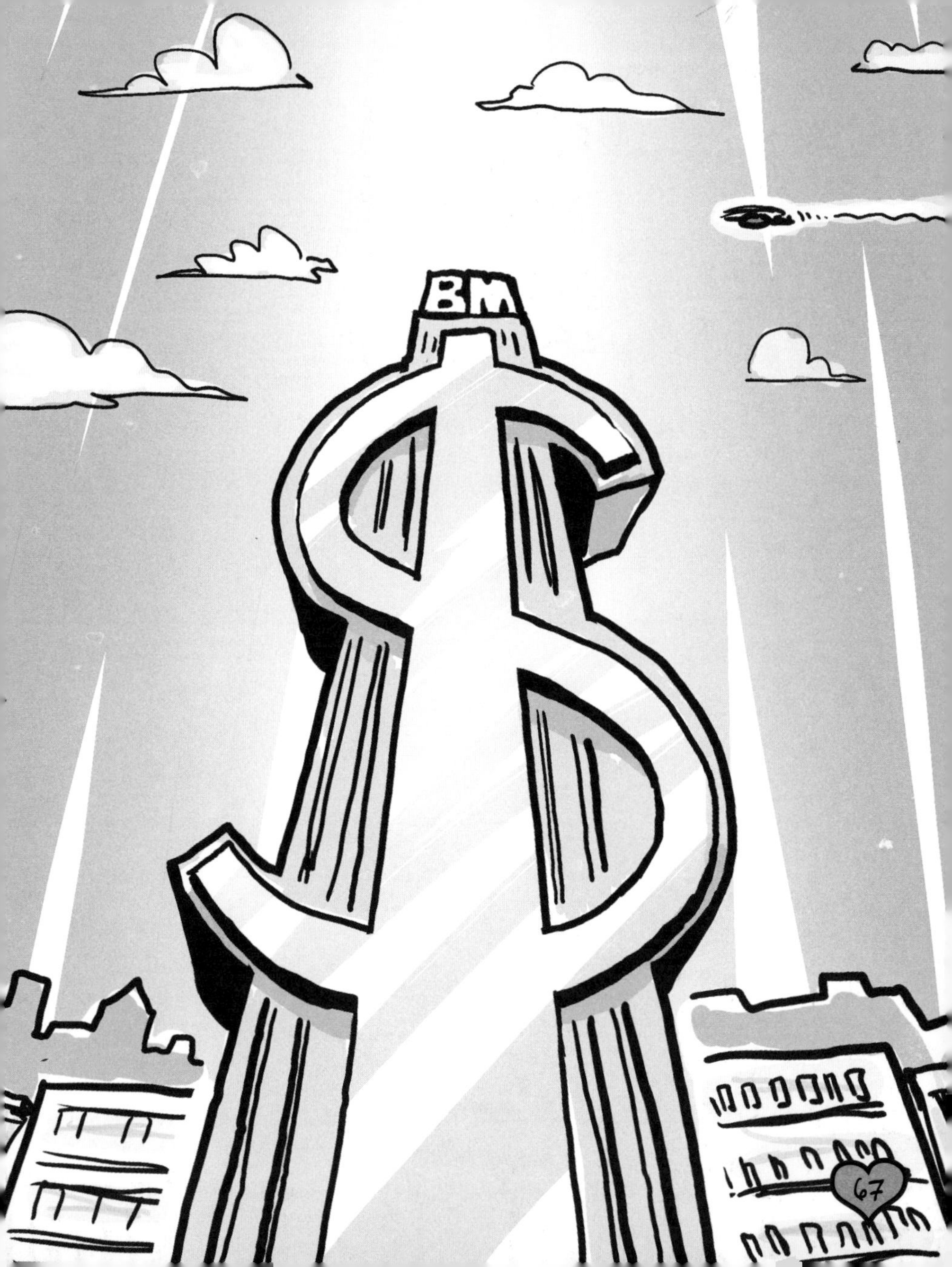
BM

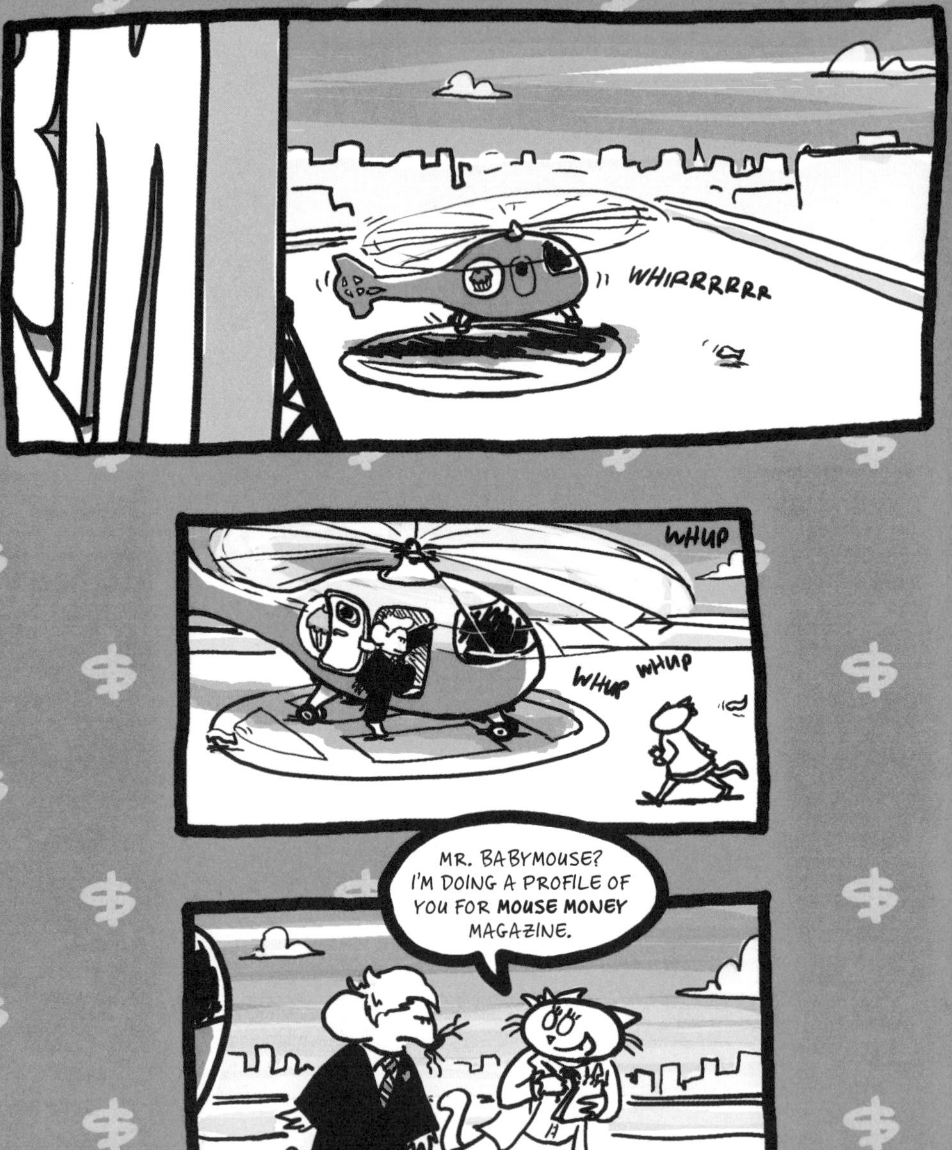
WHIRRRRRR
WHUP
WHUP WHUP
MR. BABYMOUSE? I'M DOING A PROFILE OF YOU FOR **MOUSE MONEY** MAGAZINE.

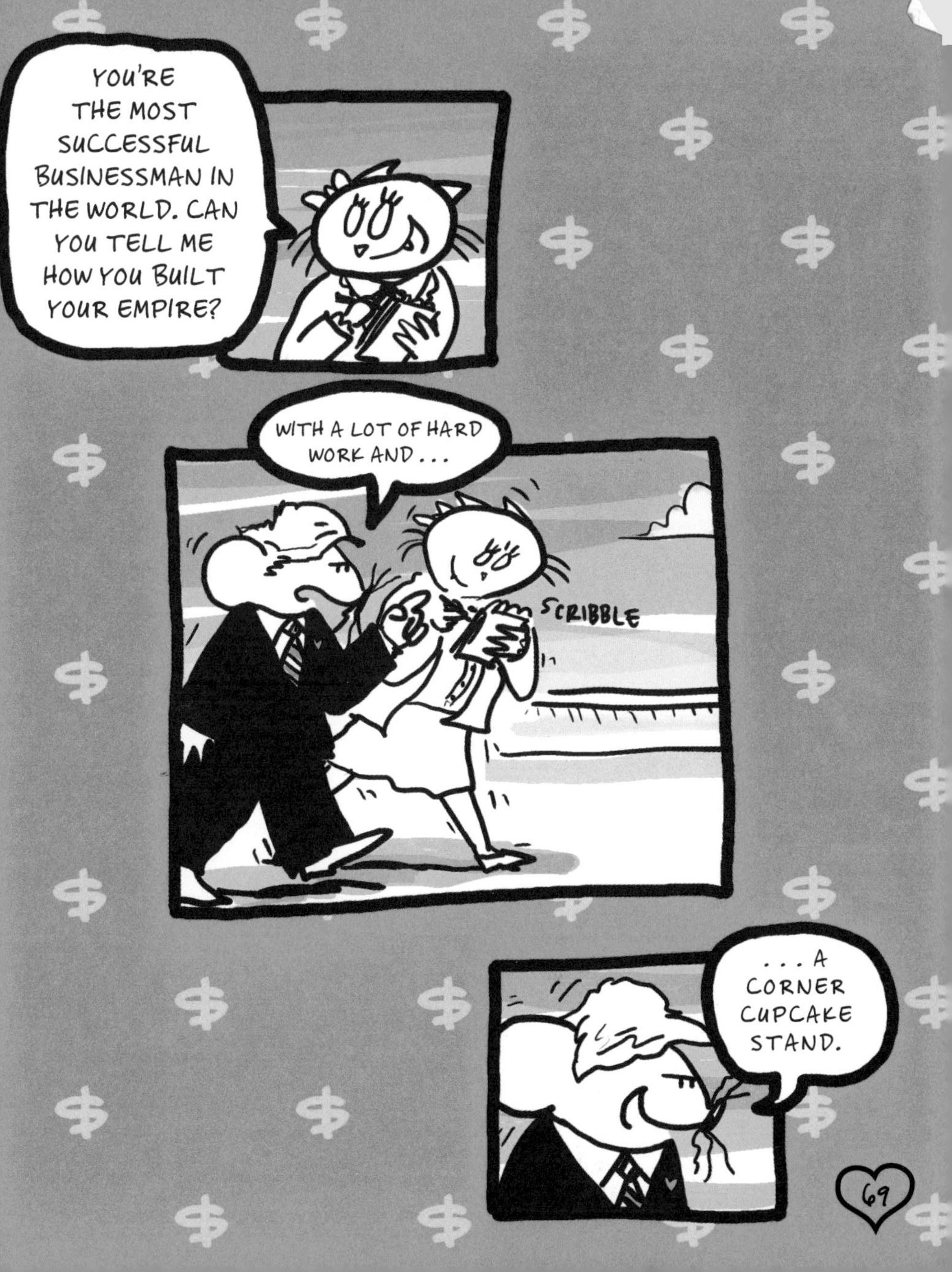

YOU'RE THE MOST SUCCESSFUL BUSINESSMAN IN THE WORLD. CAN YOU TELL ME HOW YOU BUILT YOUR EMPIRE?
WITH A LOT OF HARD WORK AND . . .
SCRIBBLE
. . . A CORNER CUPCAKE STAND.

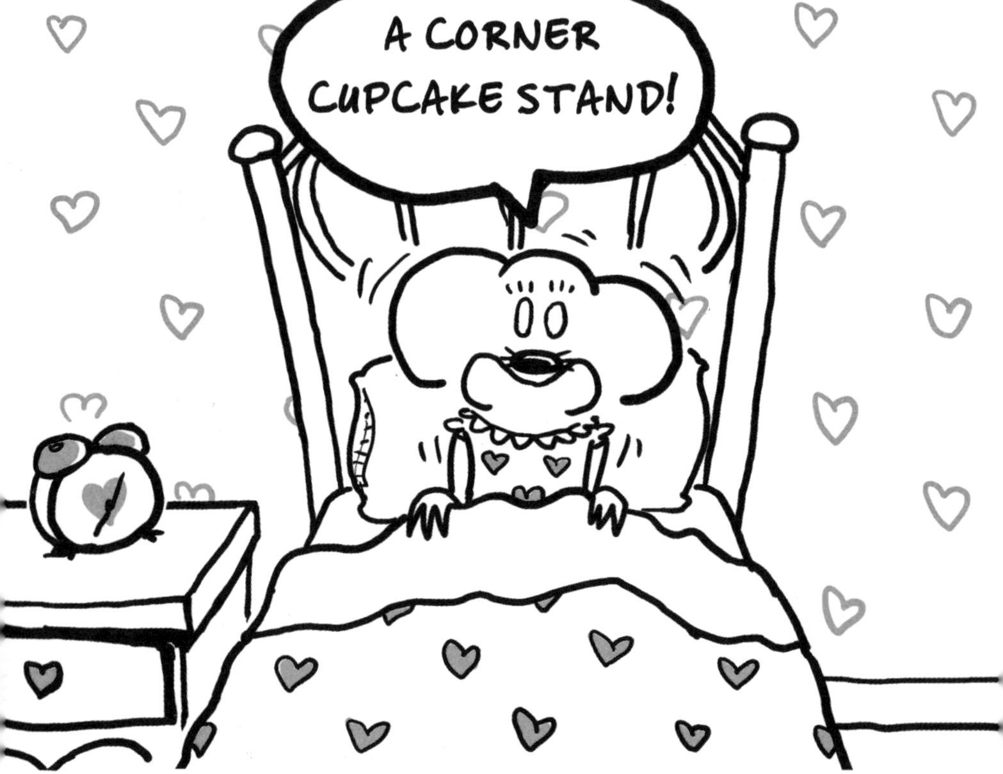
A CORNER CUPCAKE STAND!

OPERATION: CUPCAKE STAND

1 CHOOSE LOCATION!

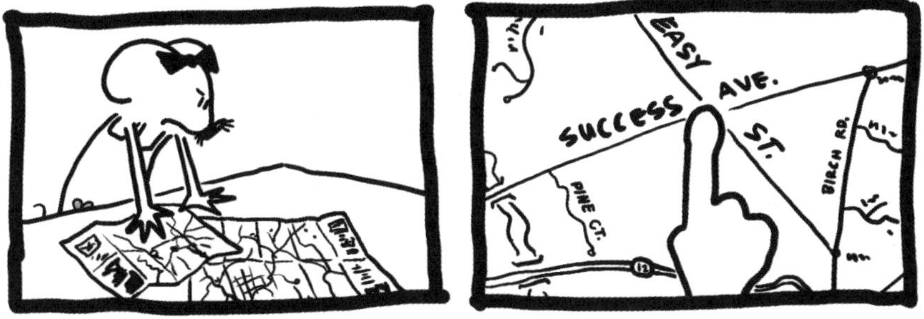
EASY
AVE.
SUCCESS
ST.
BIRCH RD.
PINE CT.

2 WRITE CLEVER SLOGAN!

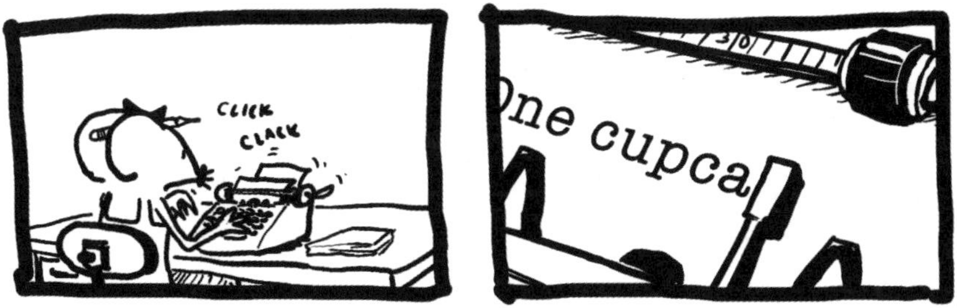
CLICK
CLACK
ne cupca

3 BUILD STOREFRONT!

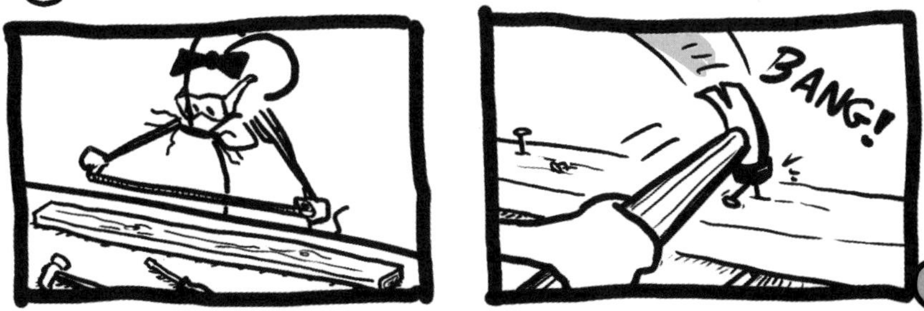
BANG!

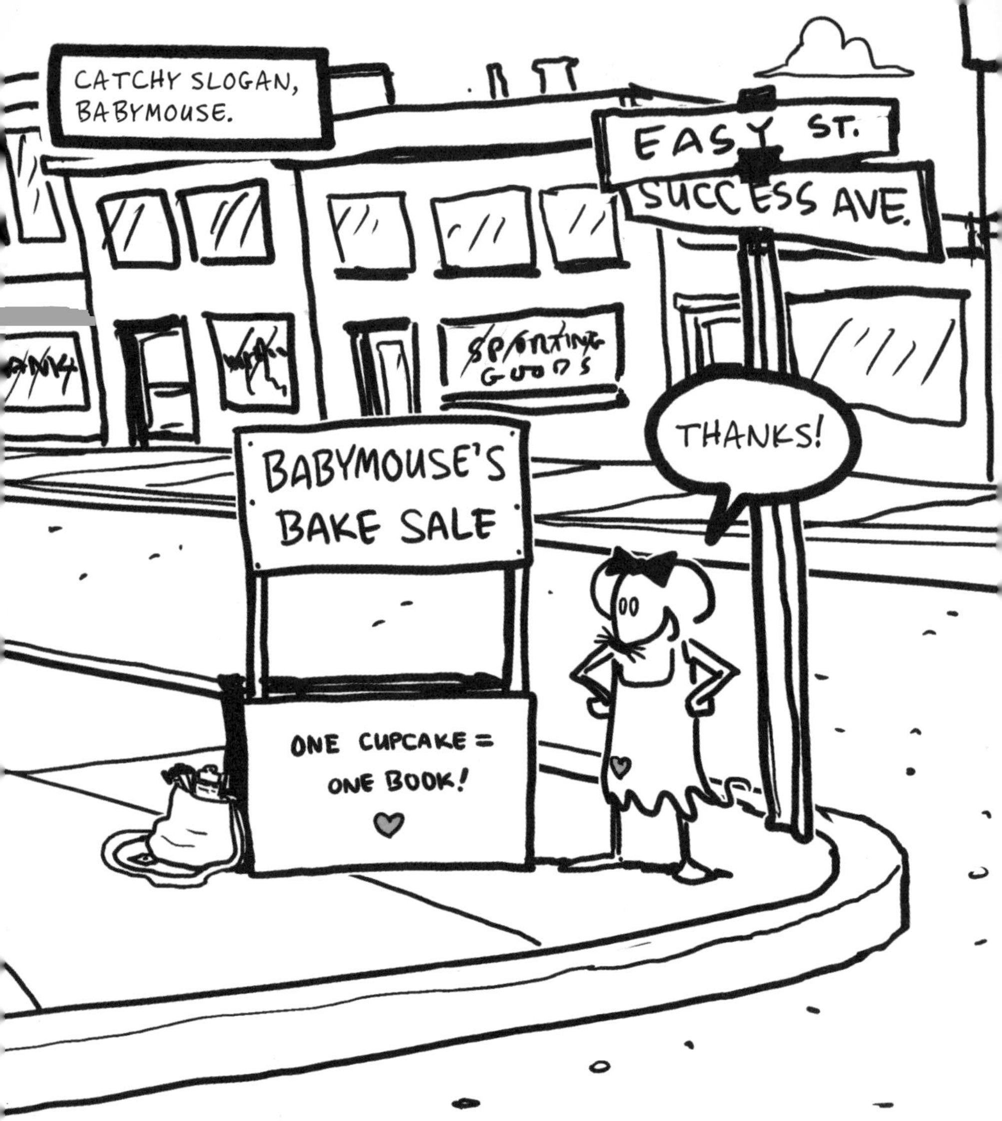

CATCHY SLOGAN, BABYMOUSE.
EASY ST.
SUCCESS AVE.
SPORTING GOODS
THANKS!
BABYMOUSE'S BAKE SALE
ONE CUPCAKE = ONE BOOK!

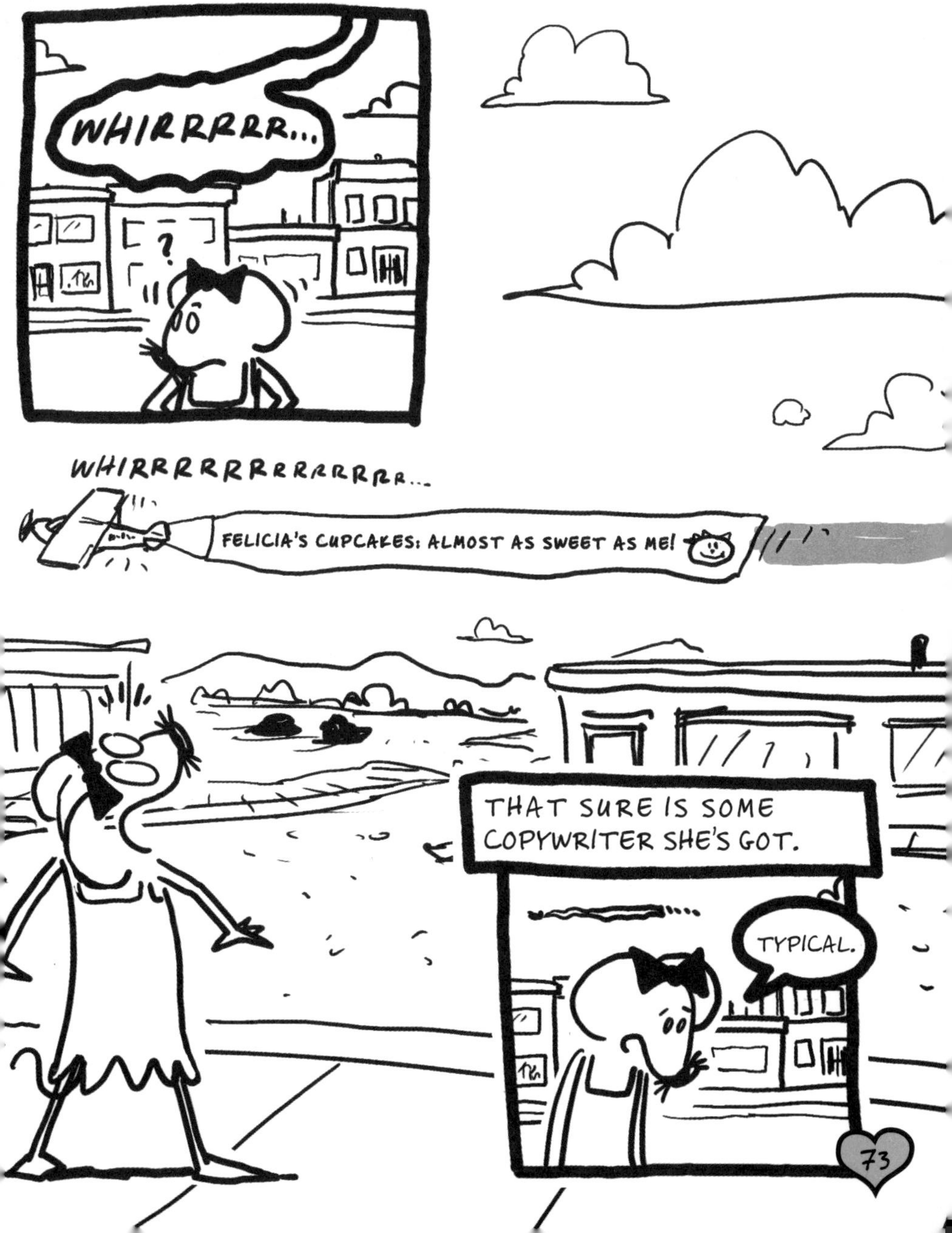
WHIRRRRR...
WHIRRRRRRRRRRRRRR...
FELICIA'S CUPCAKES: ALMOST AS SWEET AS ME!
THAT SURE IS SOME COPYWRITER SHE'S GOT.
TYPICAL.

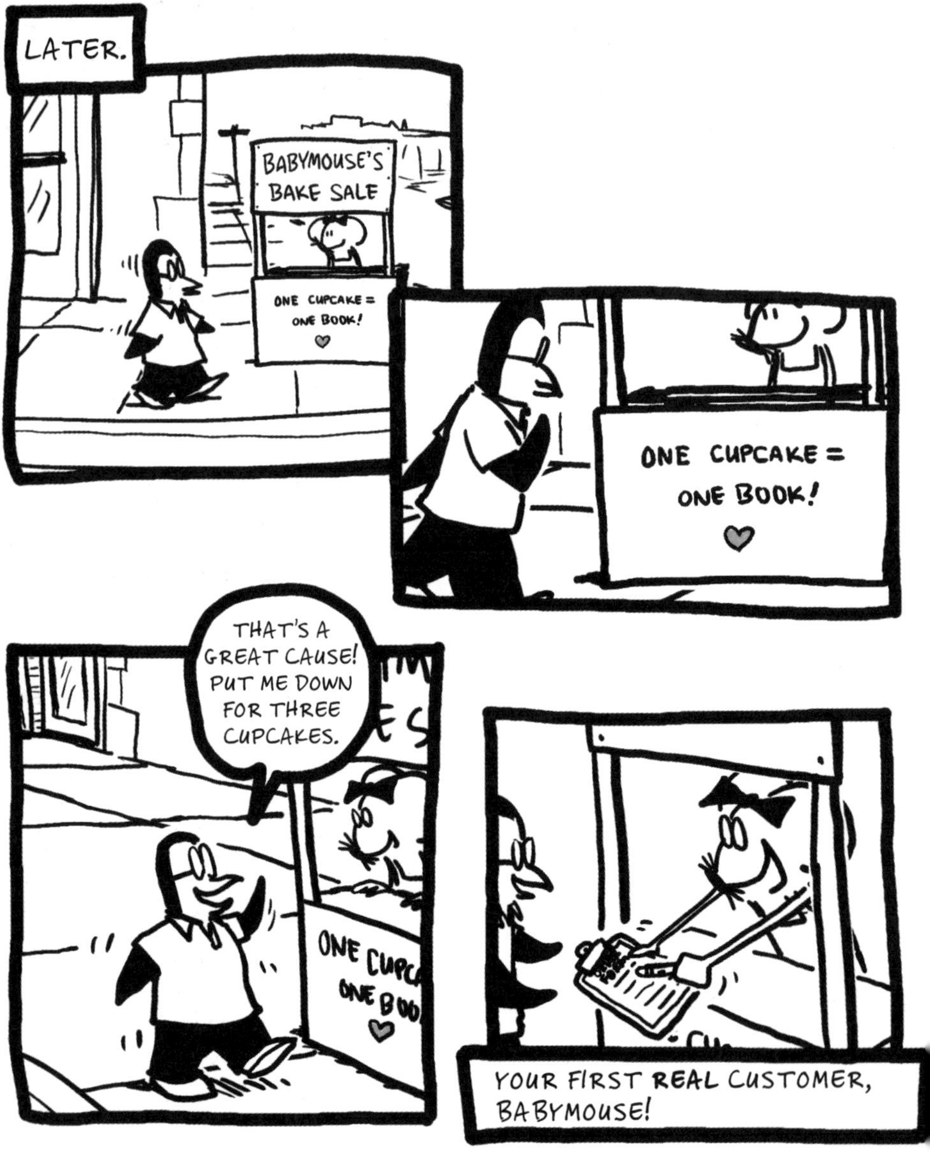
LATER.
BABYMOUSE'S BAKE SALE
ONE CUPCAKE = ONE BOOK!
ONE CUPCAKE = ONE BOOK!
THAT'S A GREAT CAUSE! PUT ME DOWN FOR THREE CUPCAKES.
YOUR FIRST **REAL** CUSTOMER, BABYMOUSE!

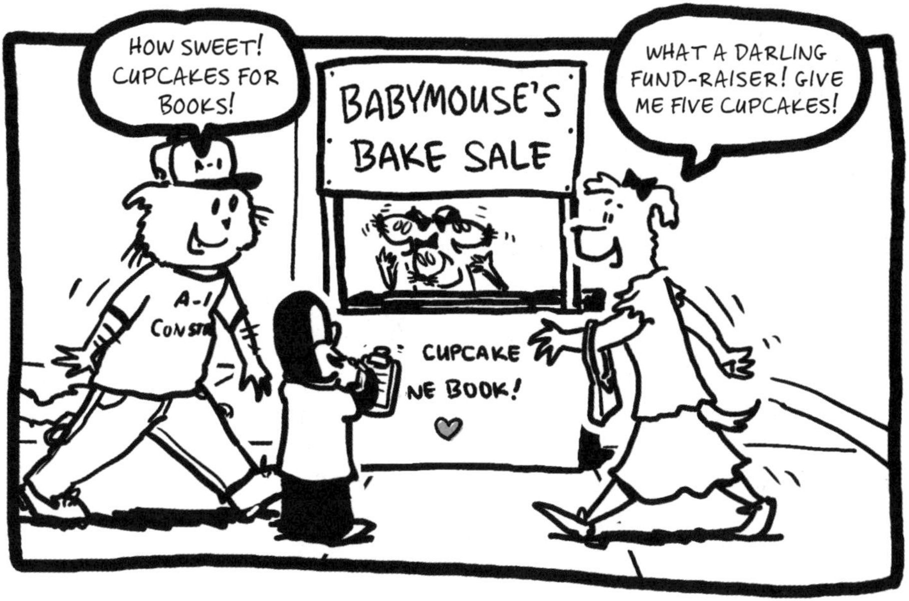
HOW SWEET! CUPCAKES FOR BOOKS!
BABYMOUSE'S BAKE SALE
WHAT A DARLING FUND-RAISER! GIVE ME FIVE CUPCAKES!
A-1 CONST
CUPCAKE
NE BOOK!

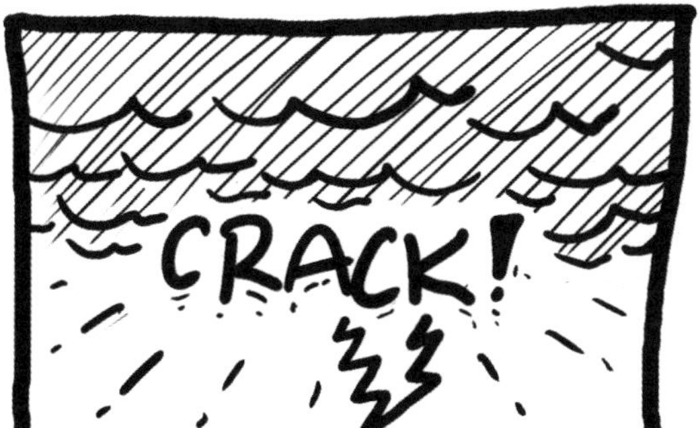
CRACK!

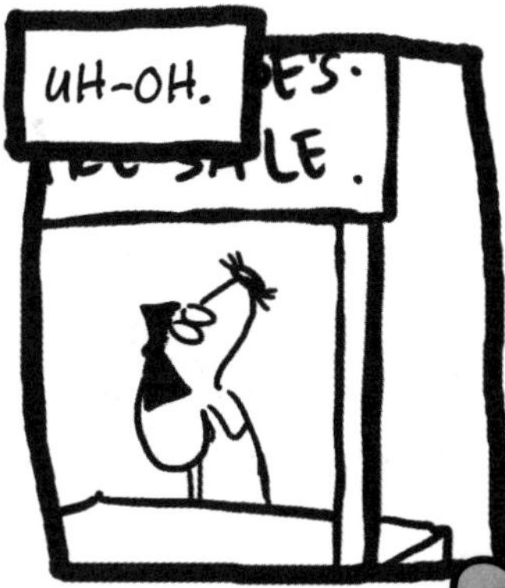
UH-OH.

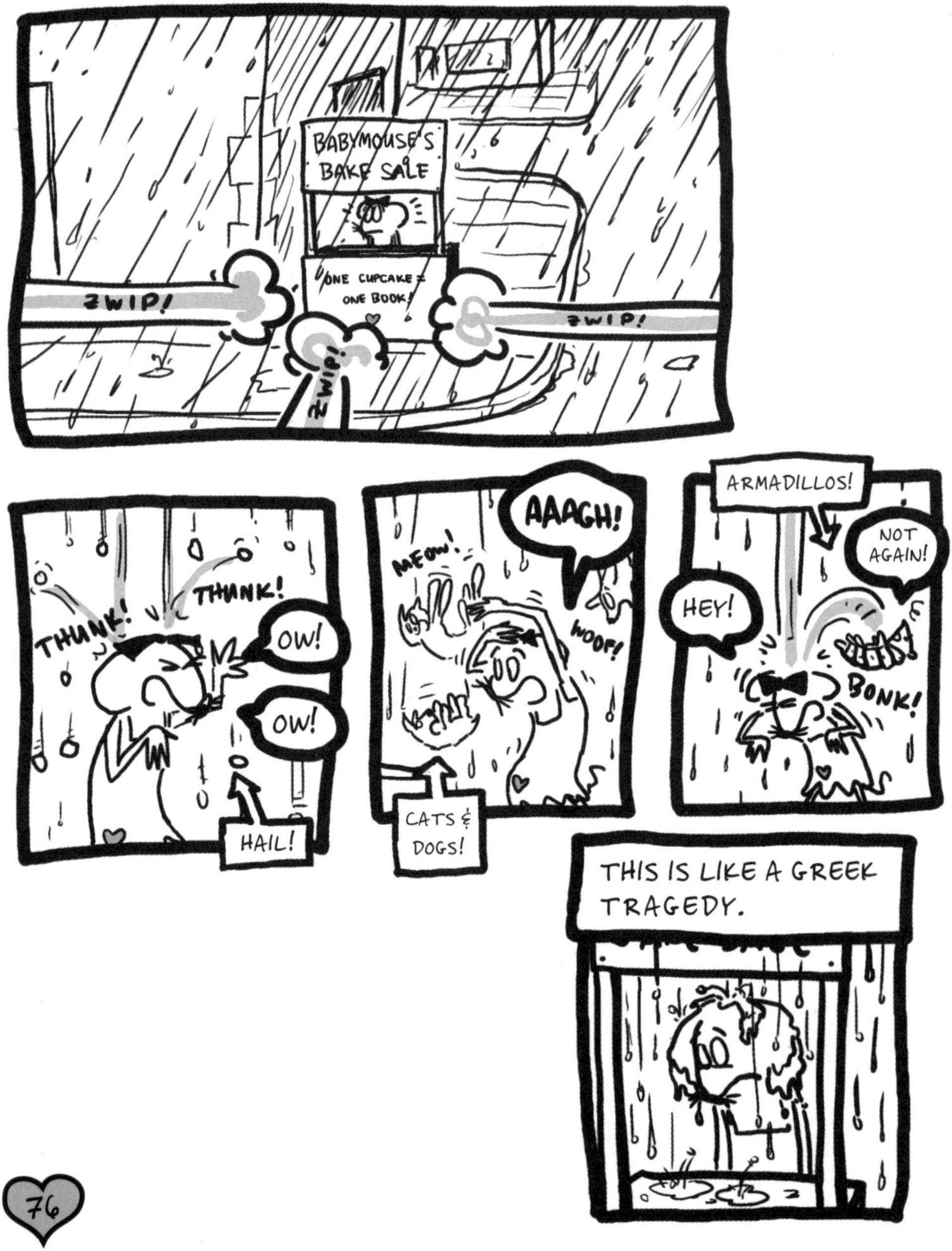

BABYMOUSE'S BAKE SALE
ONE CUPCAKE = ONE BOOK!
ZWIP!
ZWIP!
ZWIP!
THUNK!
THUNK!
OW!
OW!
HAIL!
MEOW!
AAAGH!
WOOF!
CATS & DOGS!
ARMADILLOS!
HEY!
NOT AGAIN!
BONK!
THIS IS LIKE A GREEK TRAGEDY.

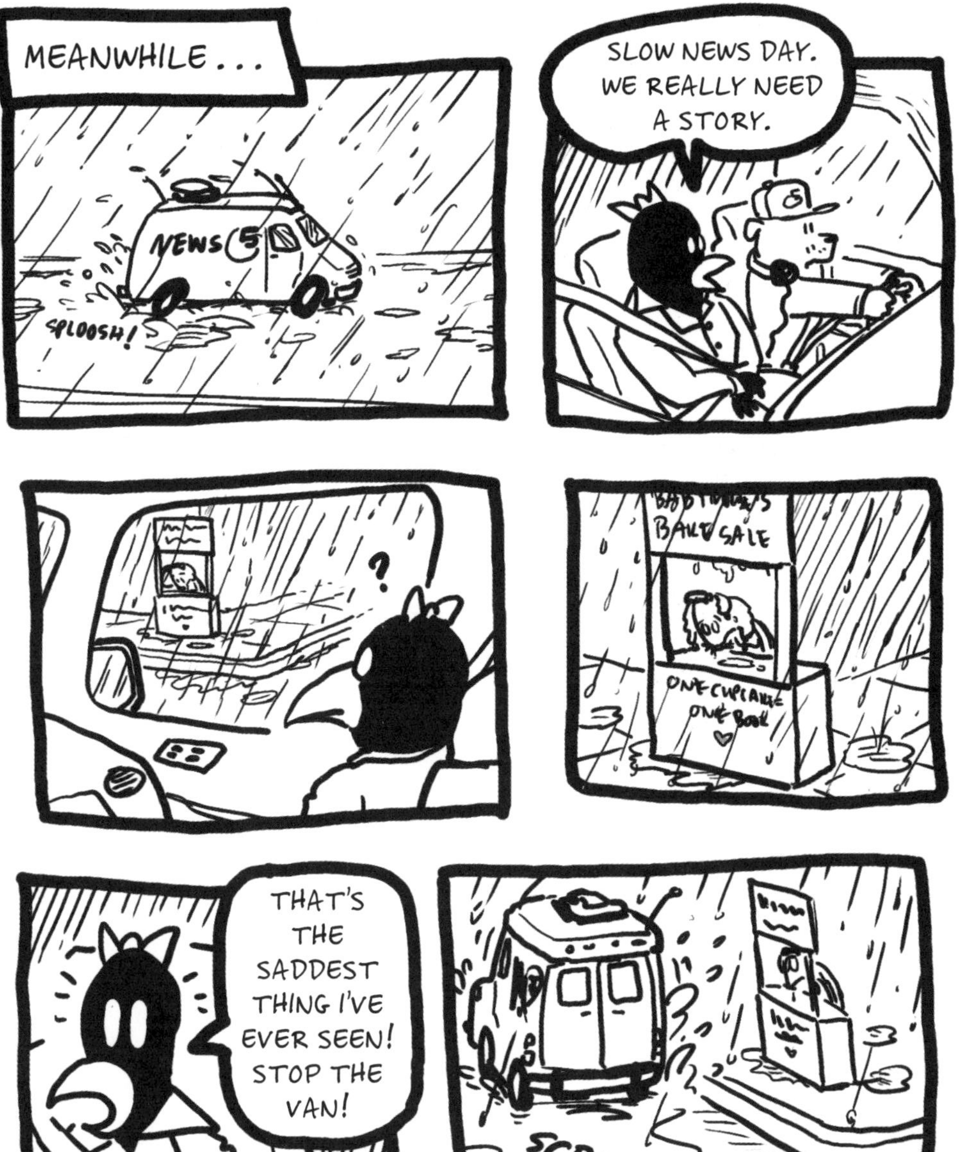
MEANWHILE . . .
NEWS 5
SPLOOSH!
SLOW NEWS DAY. WE REALLY NEED A STORY.
?
BAKE SALE
ONE CUPCAKE ONE BOOK
THAT'S THE SADDEST THING I'VE EVER SEEN! STOP THE VAN!
SCREECH!

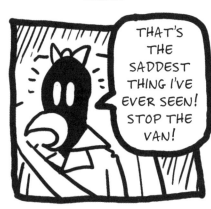

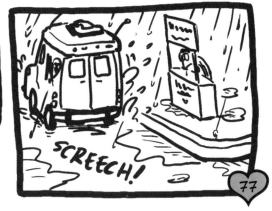

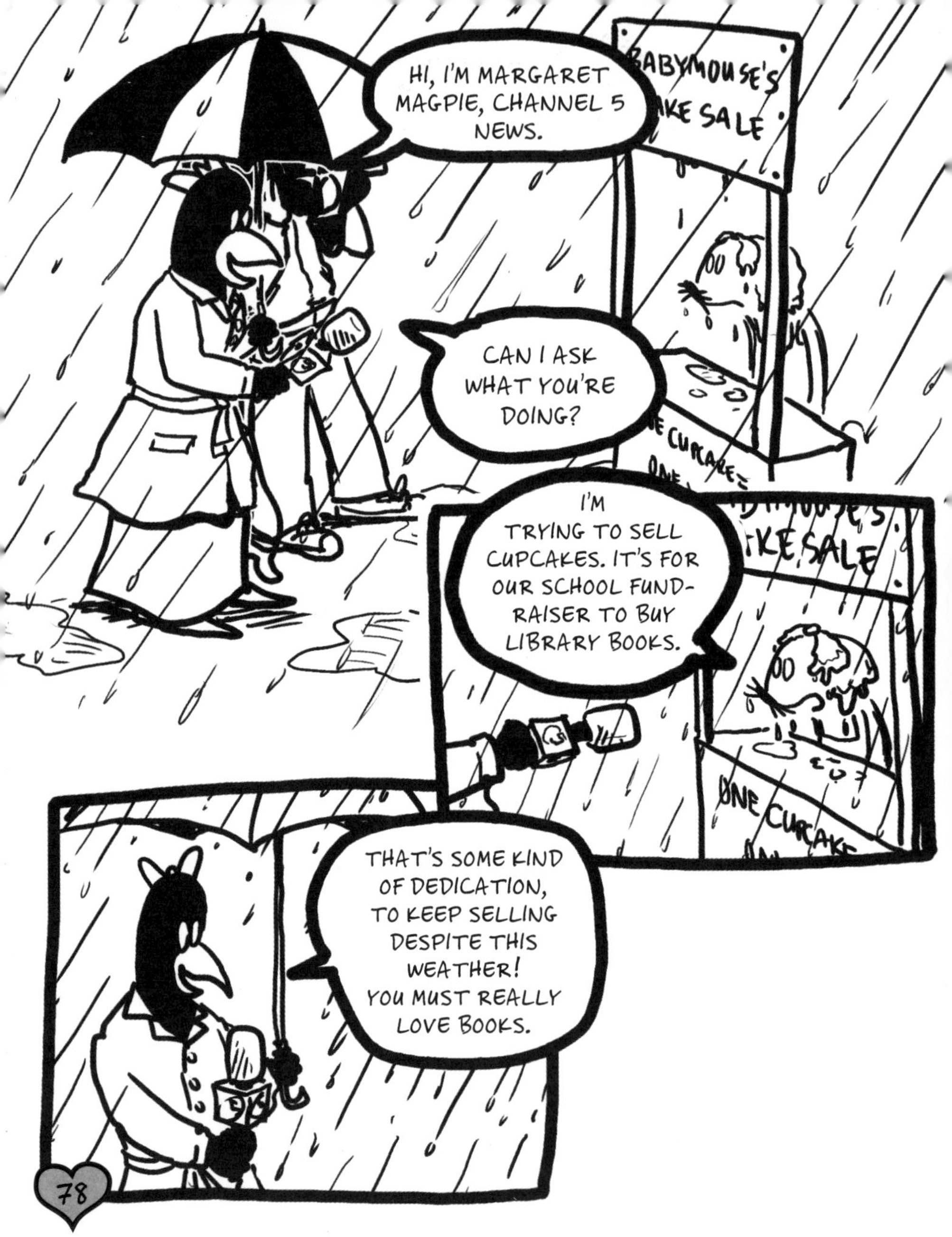

BABYMOUSE'S
...KE SALE
HI, I'M MARGARET MAGPIE, CHANNEL 5 NEWS.
CAN I ASK WHAT YOU'RE DOING?
I'M TRYING TO SELL CUPCAKES. IT'S FOR OUR SCHOOL FUND-RAISER TO BUY LIBRARY BOOKS.
ONE CUPCAKE
THAT'S SOME KIND OF DEDICATION, TO KEEP SELLING DESPITE THIS WEATHER! YOU MUST REALLY LOVE BOOKS.

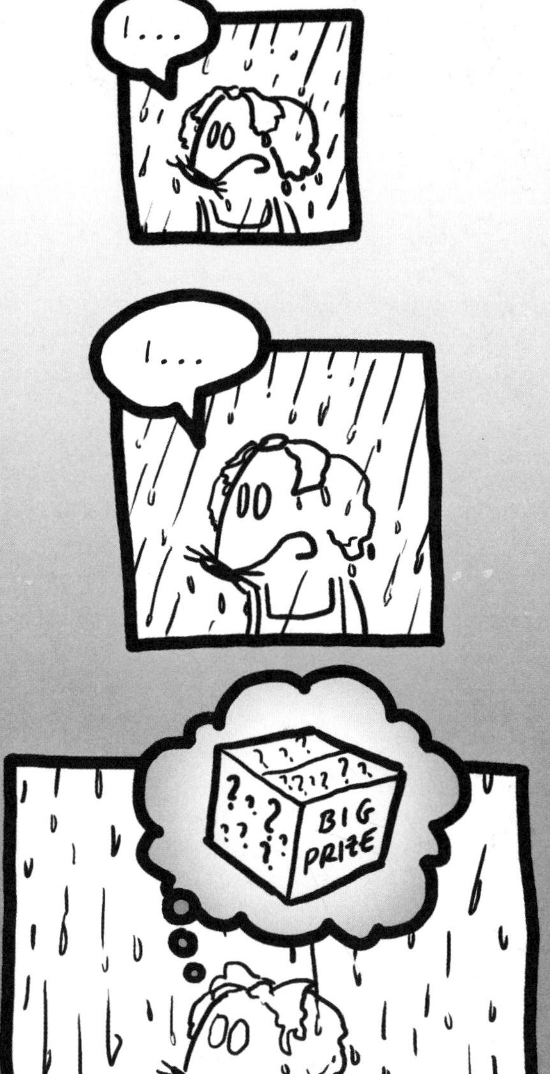
I . . .
I . . .
BIG PRIZE

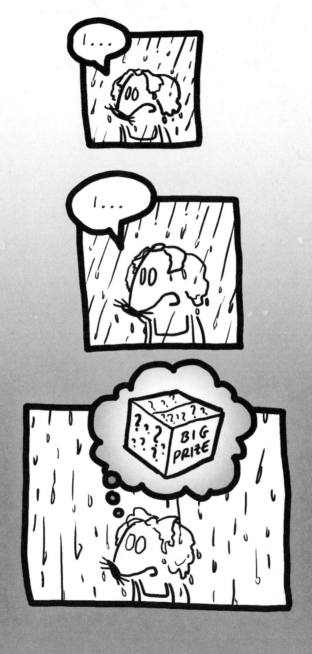

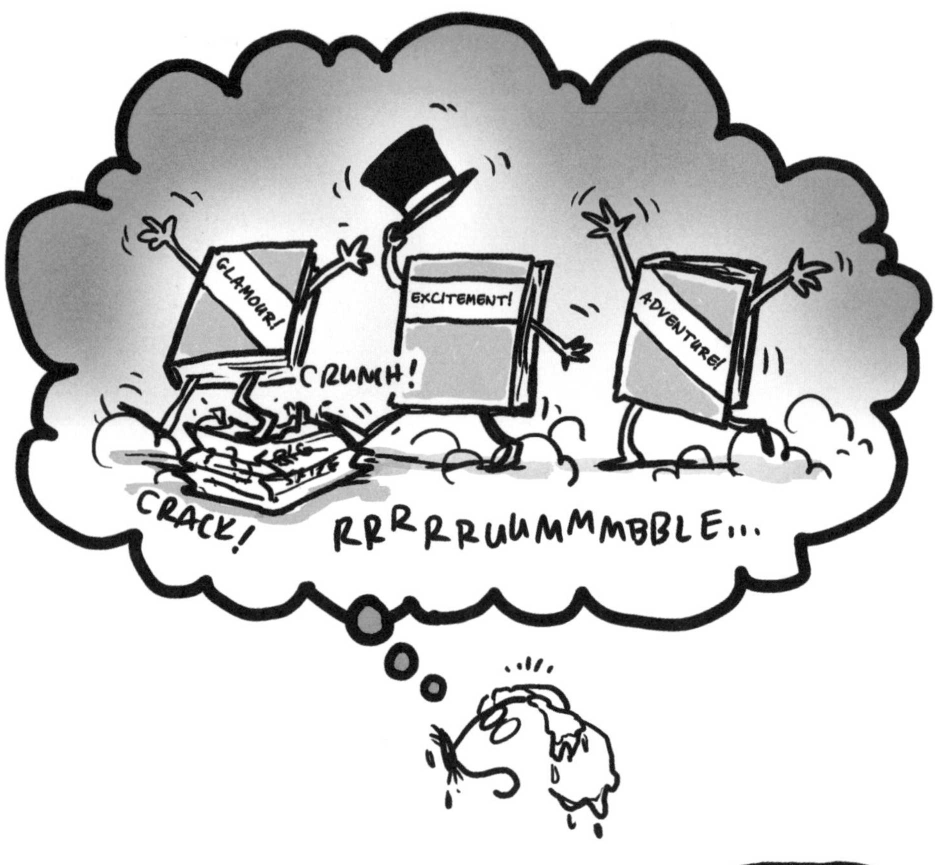
GLAMOUR!
EXCITEMENT!
ADVENTURE!
CRUNCH!
CRACK!
RRRRRUUMMMMBBLE...

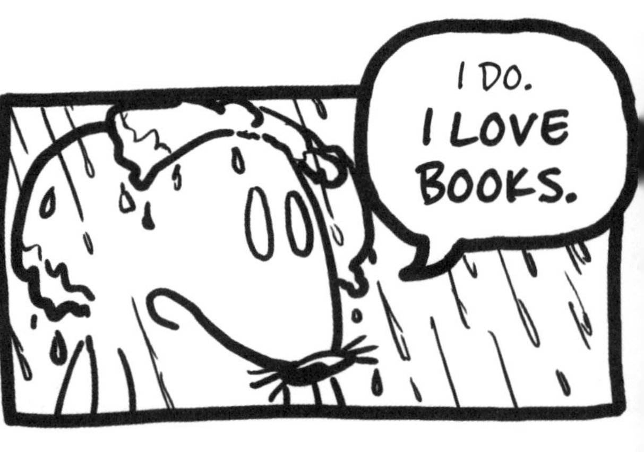
I DO.
I LOVE BOOKS.

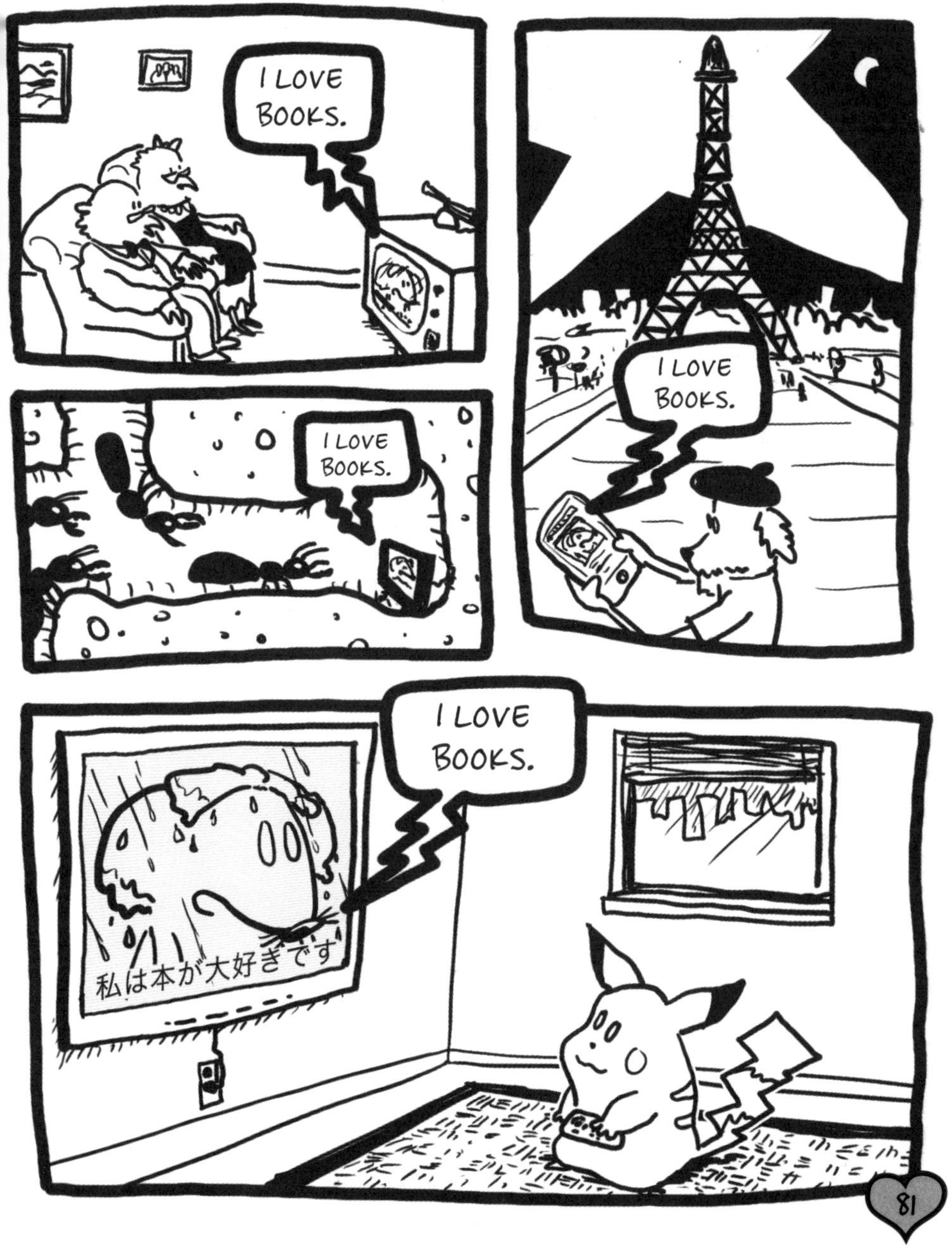
I LOVE BOOKS.
I LOVE BOOKS.
I LOVE BOOKS.
I LOVE BOOKS.
私は本が大好きです

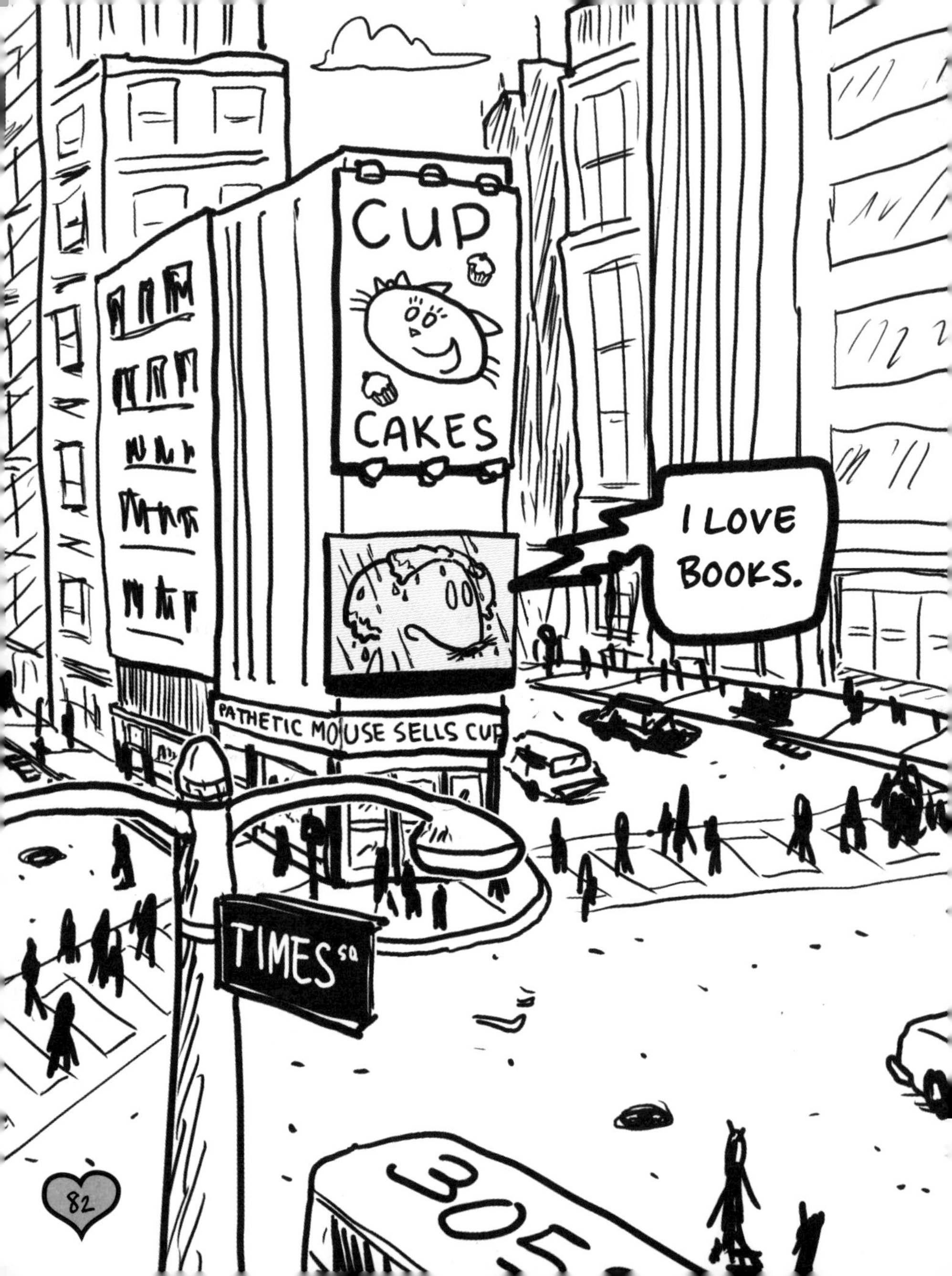
CUP CAKES
I LOVE BOOKS.
PATHETIC MOUSE SELLS CUP
TIMES SQ
305

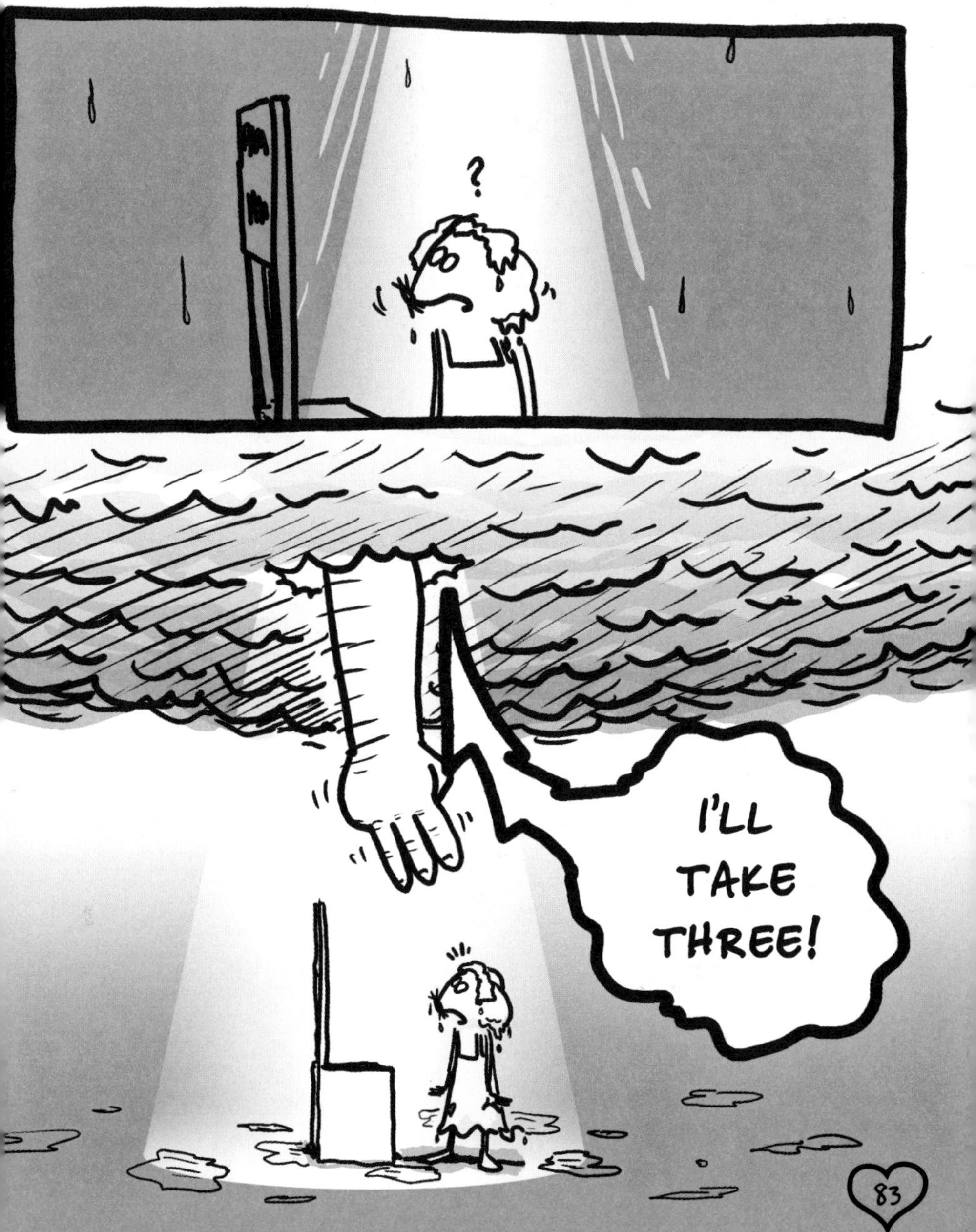
?
I'LL TAKE THREE!

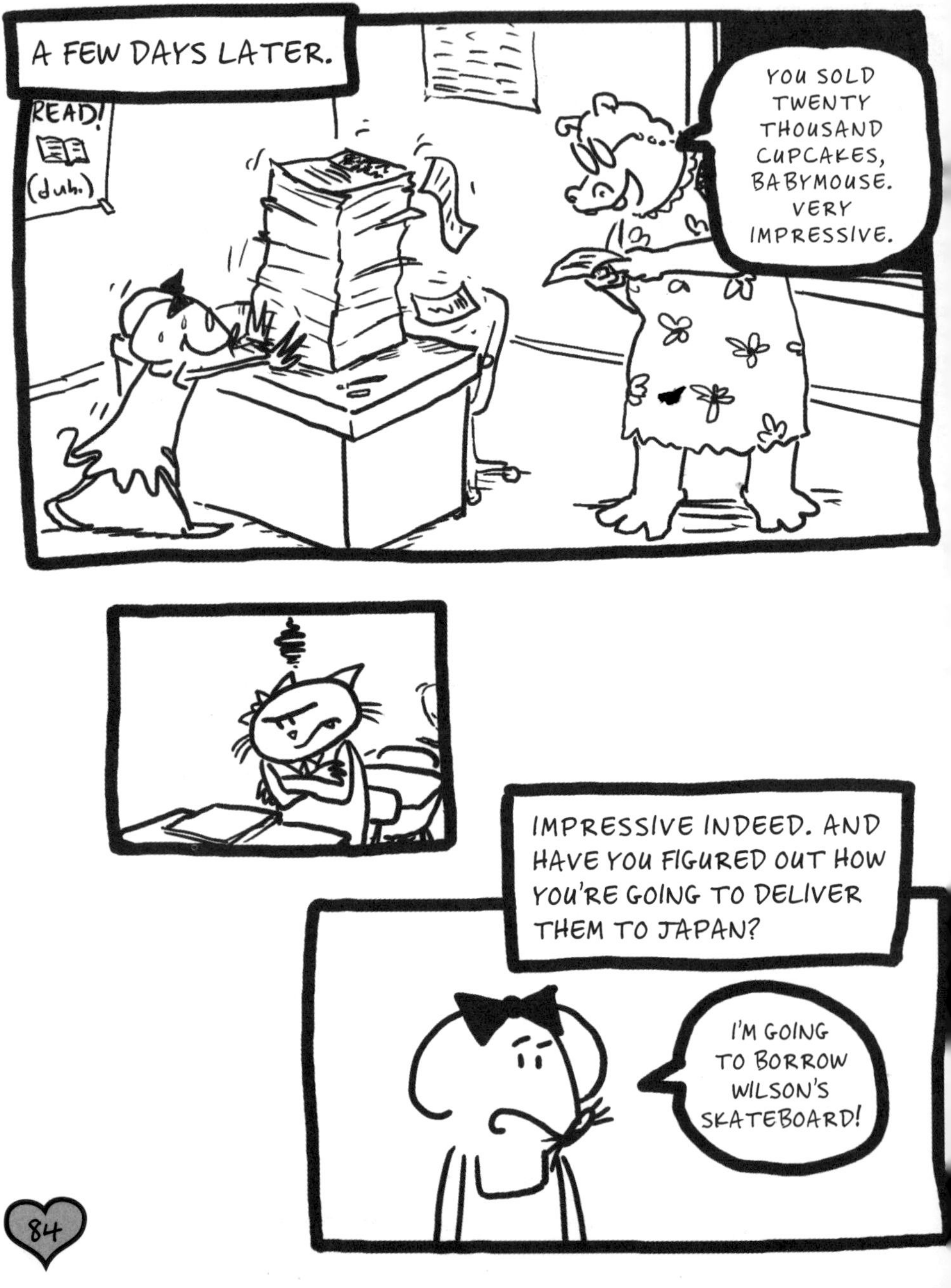

A FEW DAYS LATER.
READ! (duh.)
YOU SOLD TWENTY THOUSAND CUPCAKES, BABYMOUSE. VERY IMPRESSIVE.
IMPRESSIVE INDEED. AND HAVE YOU FIGURED OUT HOW YOU'RE GOING TO DELIVER THEM TO JAPAN?
I'M GOING TO BORROW WILSON'S SKATEBOARD!

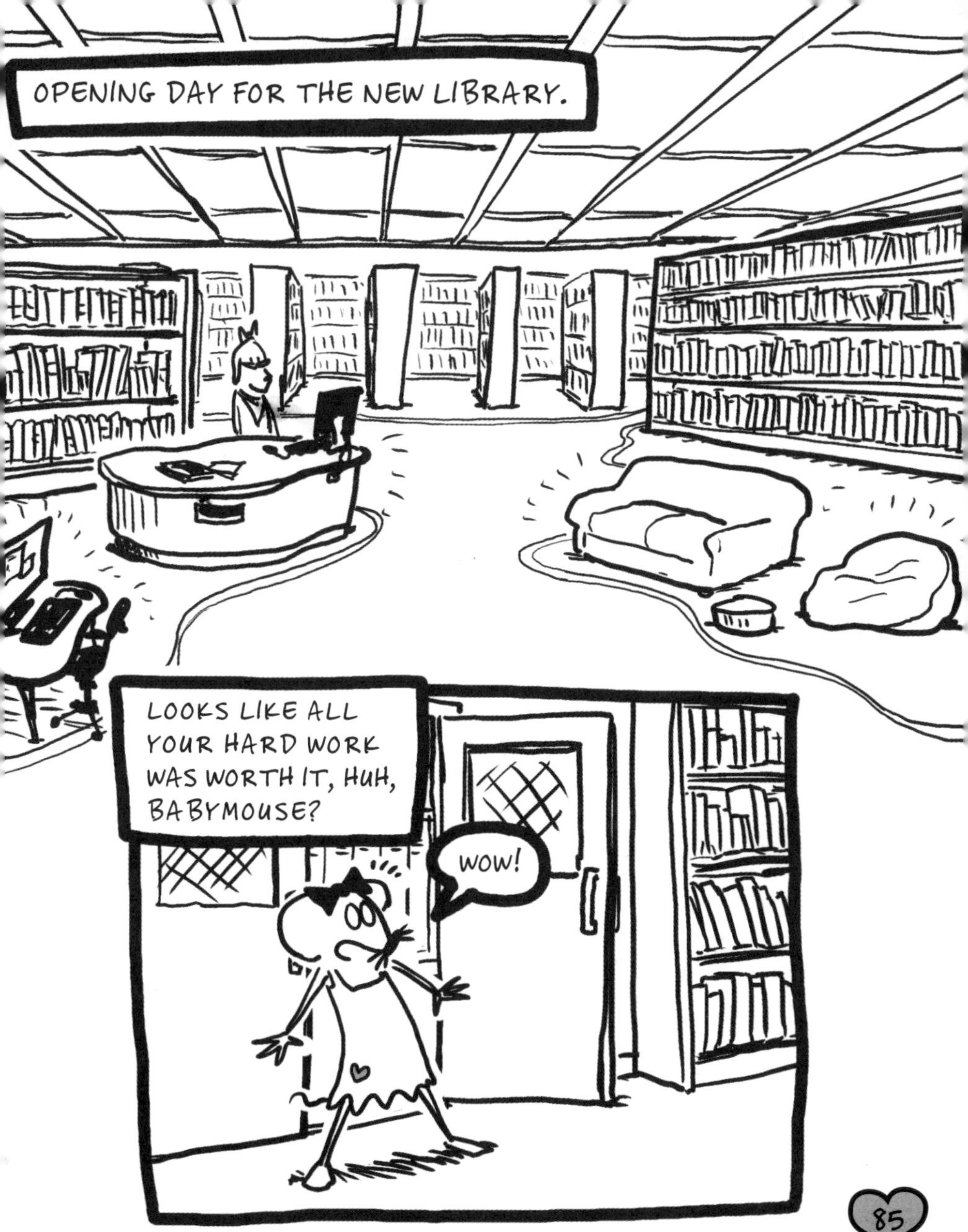

OPENING DAY FOR THE NEW LIBRARY.
LOOKS LIKE ALL YOUR HARD WORK WAS WORTH IT, HUH, BABYMOUSE?
WOW!

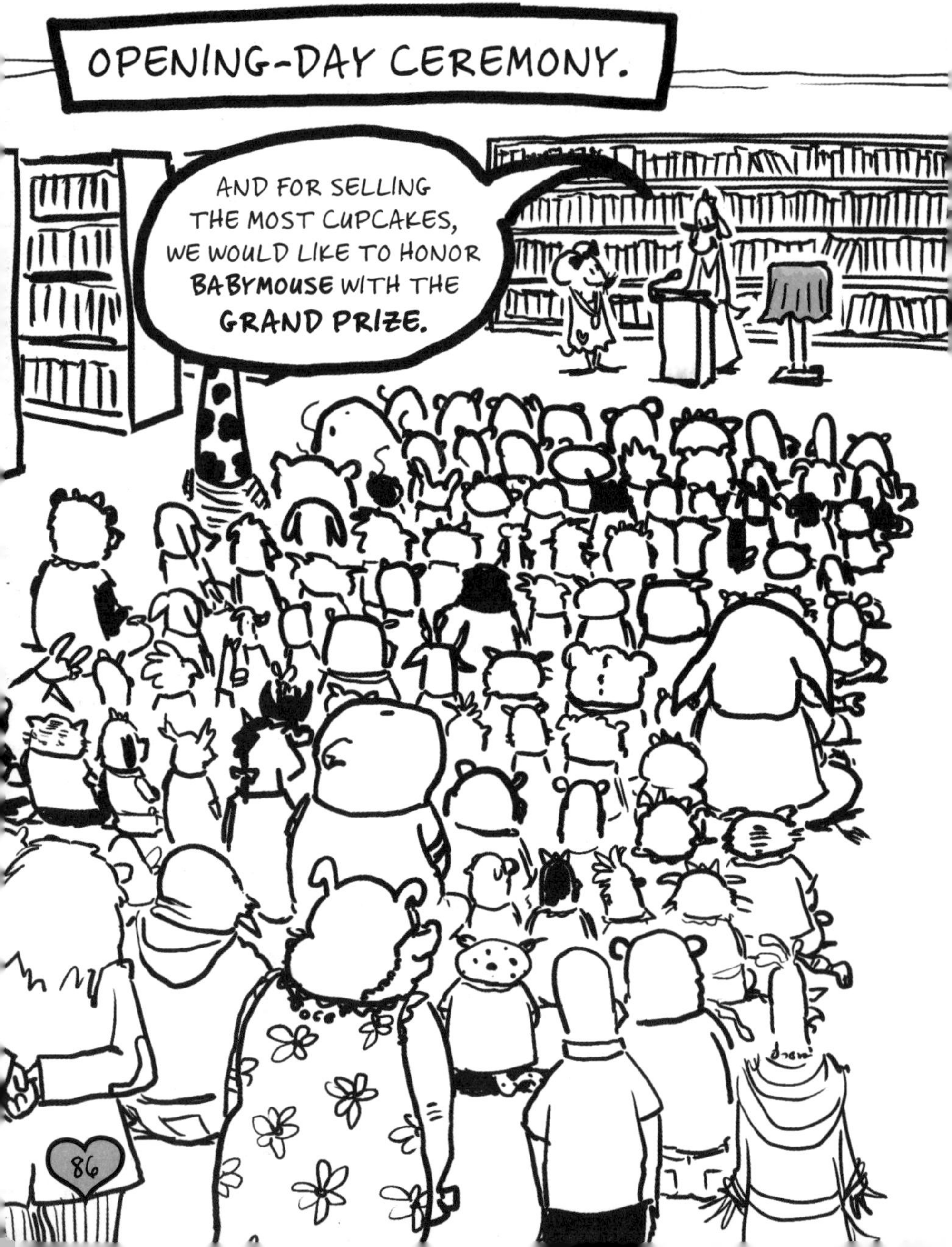
OPENING-DAY CEREMONY.
AND FOR SELLING THE MOST CUPCAKES, WE WOULD LIKE TO HONOR BABYMOUSE WITH THE GRAND PRIZE.

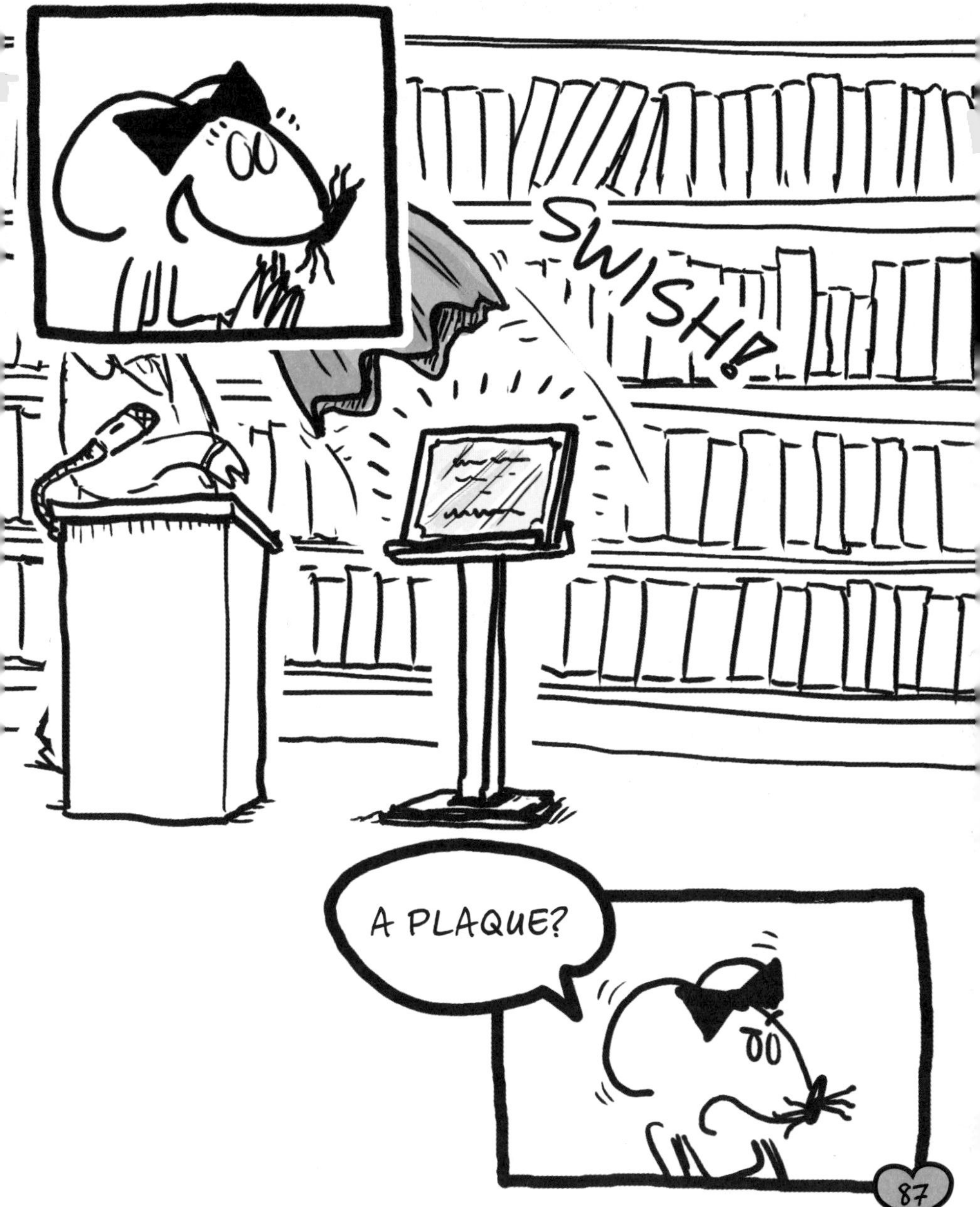
SWISH!
A PLAQUE?

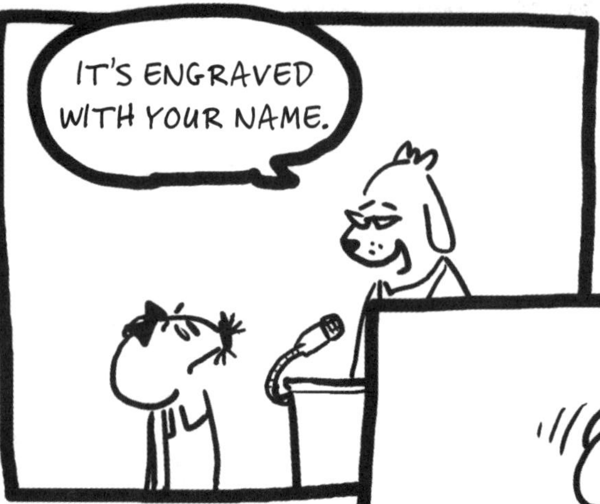
IT'S ENGRAVED
WITH YOUR NAME.

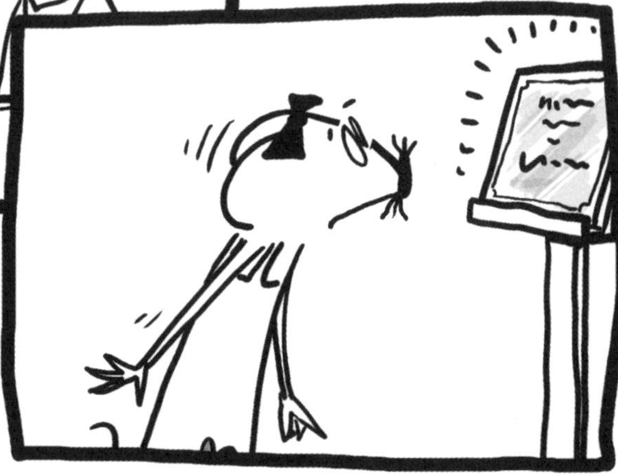

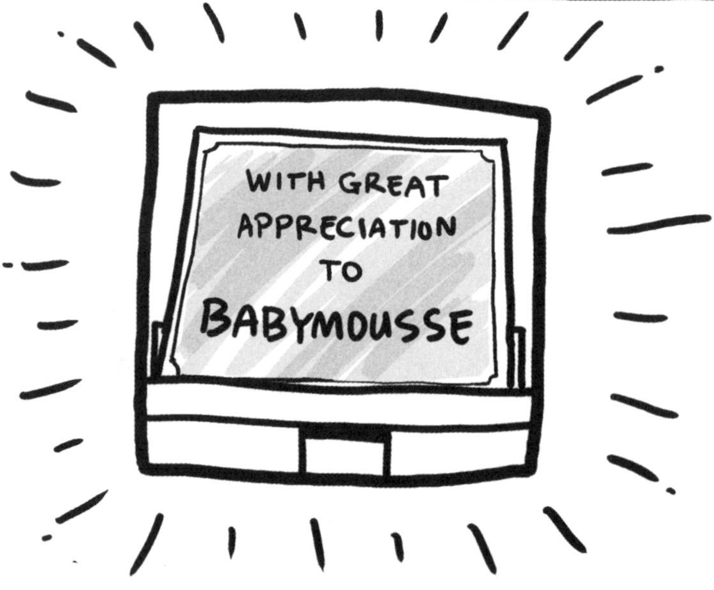
WITH GREAT
APPRECIATION
TO
BABYMOUSSE

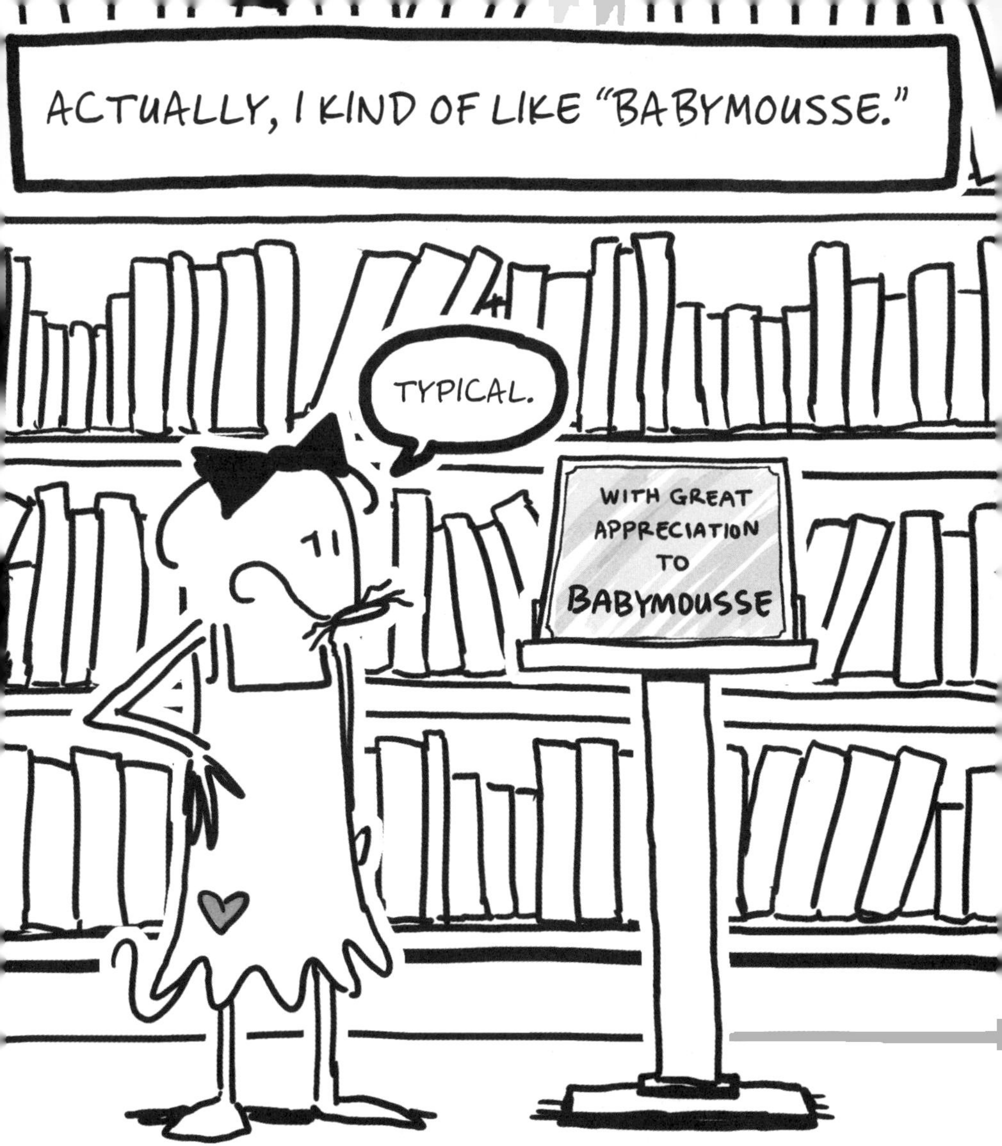
ACTUALLY, I KIND OF LIKE "BABYMOUSSE."
TYPICAL.
WITH GREAT APPRECIATION TO BABYMOUSSE

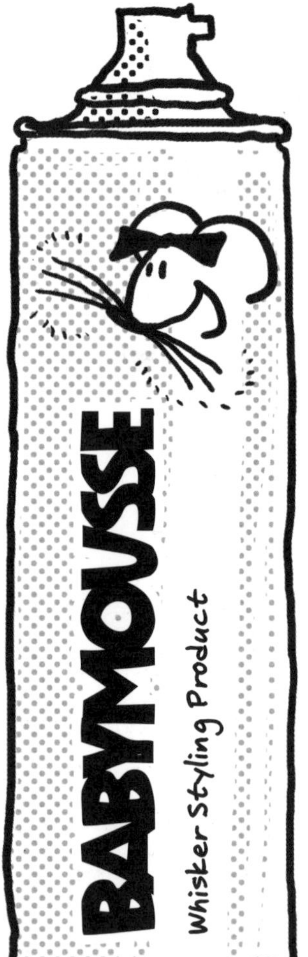
BABYMOUSSE
Whisker Styling Product

FOR PERFECT
WHISKERS
EVERY TIME!

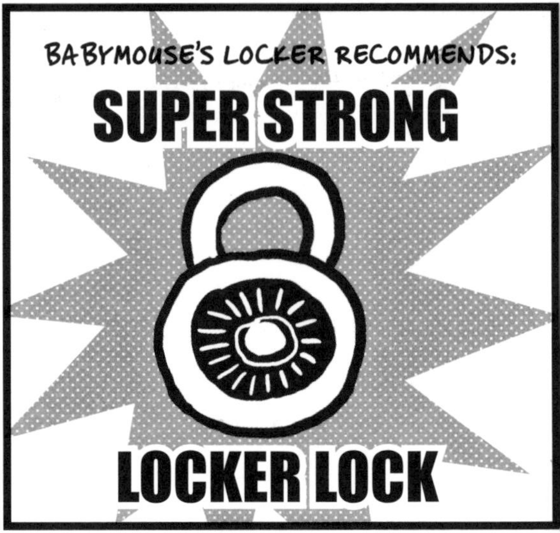
BABYMOUSE'S LOCKER RECOMMENDS:
SUPER STRONG
LOCKER LOCK

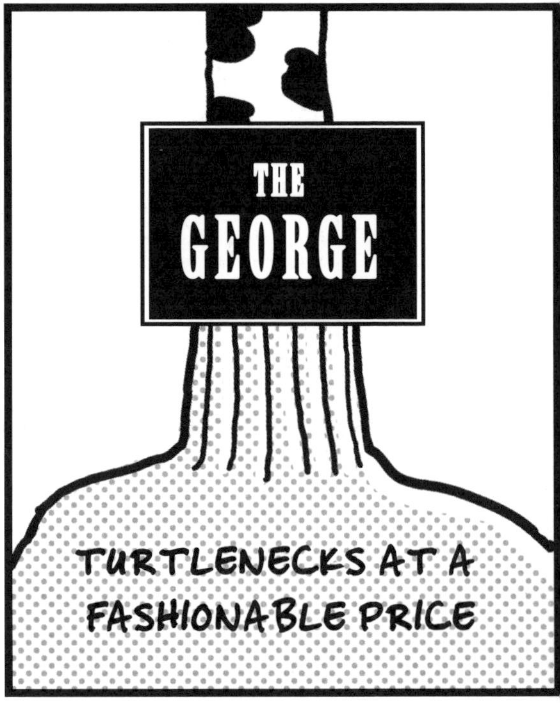
THE
GEORGE
TURTLENECKS AT A
FASHIONABLE PRICE

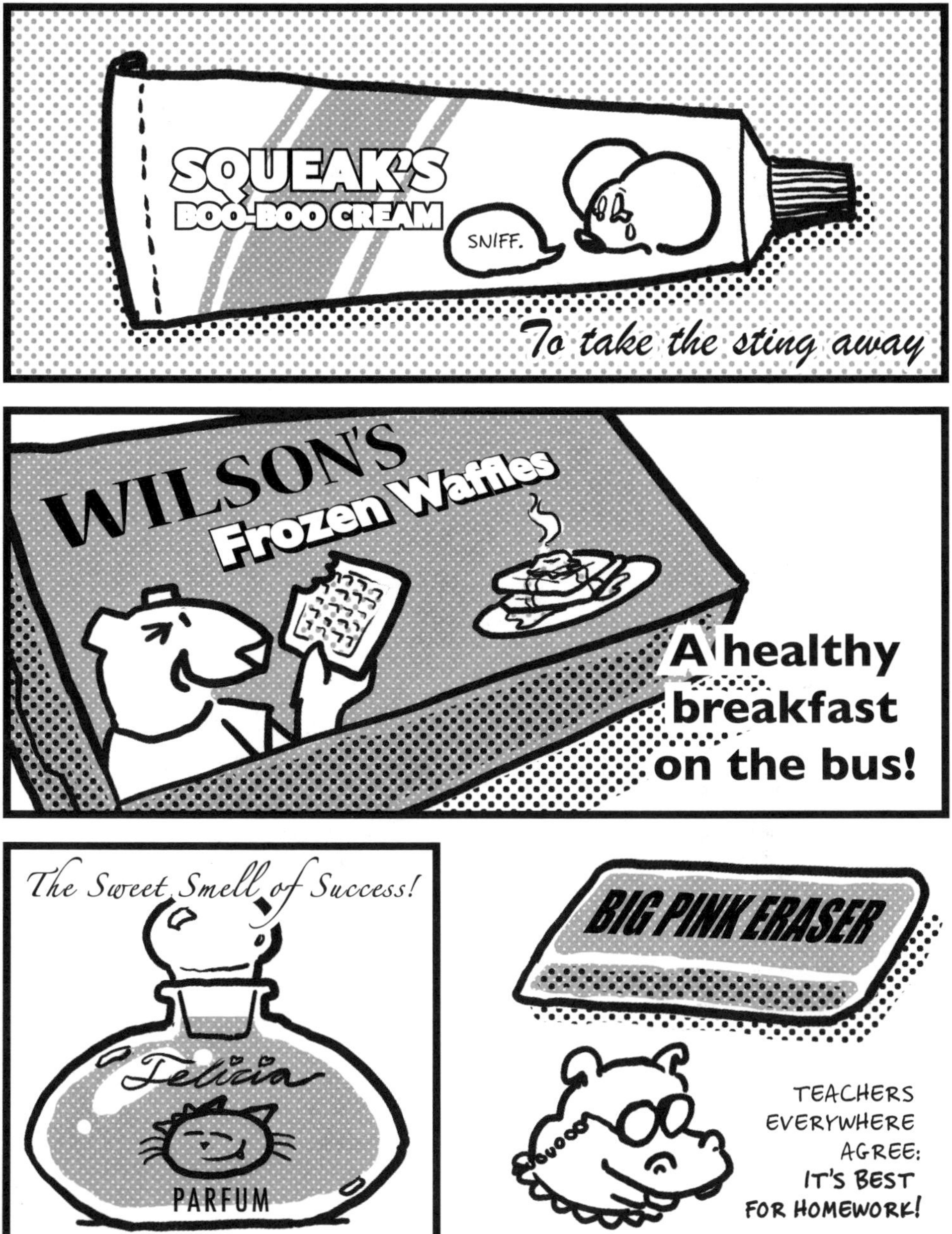
SQUEAK'S
BOO-BOO CREAM
SNIFF.
To take the sting away
WILSON'S
Frozen Waffles
A healthy
breakfast
on the bus!
The Sweet Smell of Success!
Felicia
PARFUM
BIG PINK ERASER
TEACHERS
EVERYWHERE
AGREE:
IT'S BEST
FOR HOMEWORK!

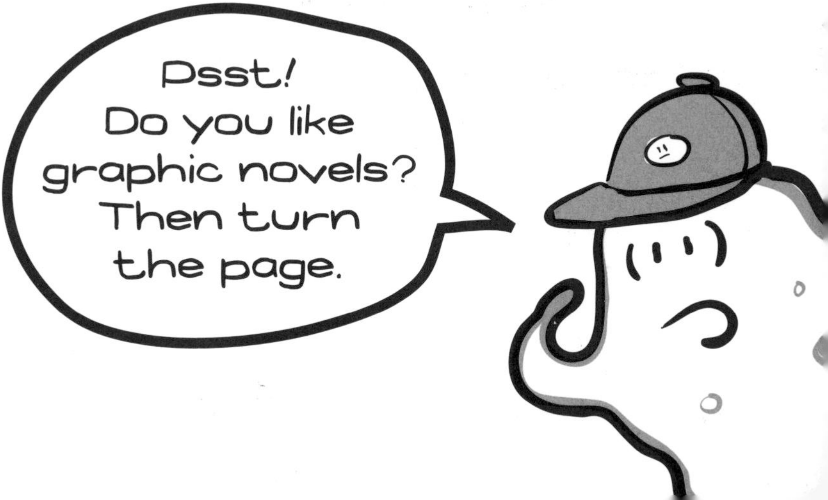
Psst!
Do you like
graphic novels?
Then turn
the page.

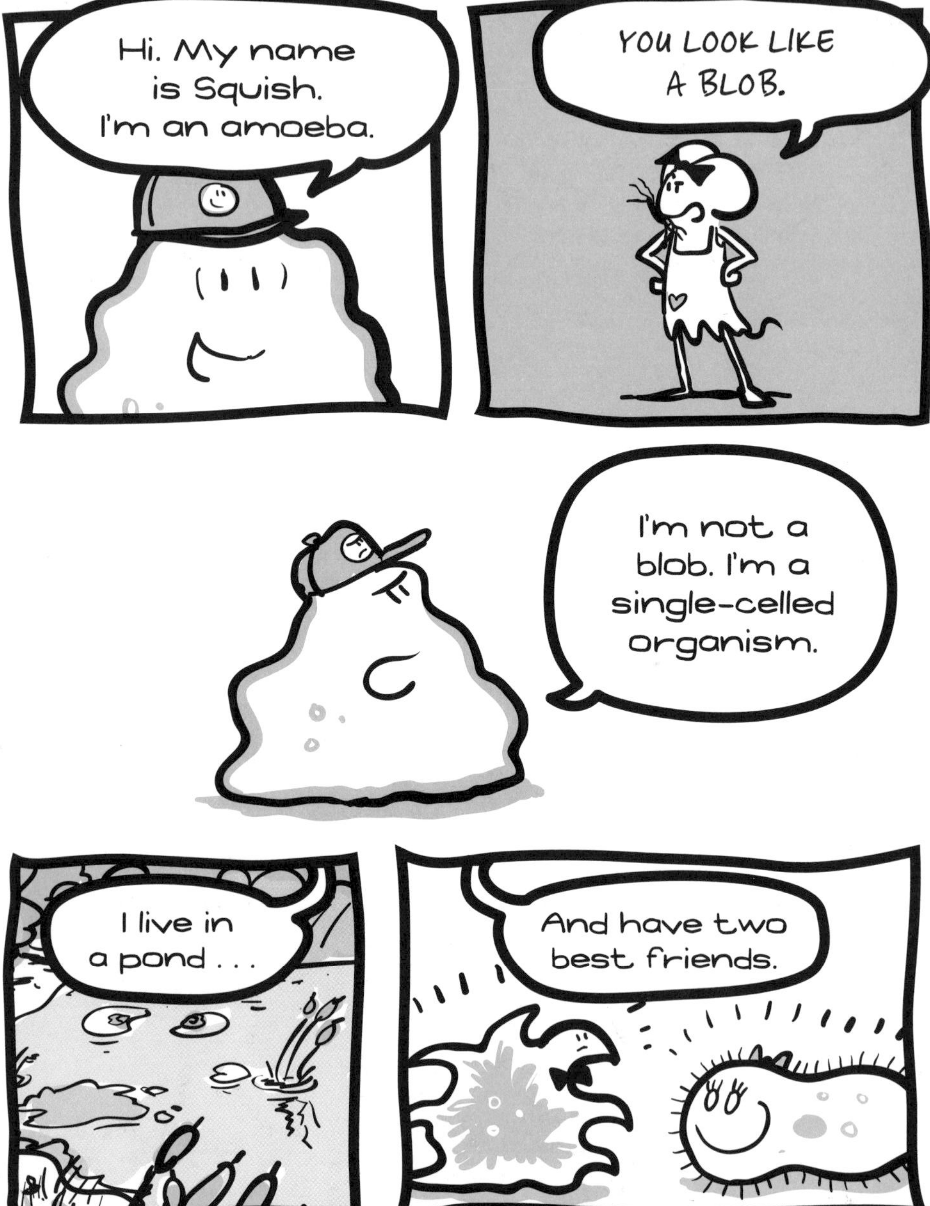
Hi. My name is Squish. I'm an amoeba.
YOU LOOK LIKE A BLOB.
I'm not a blob. I'm a single-celled organism.
I live in a pond . . .
And have two best friends.

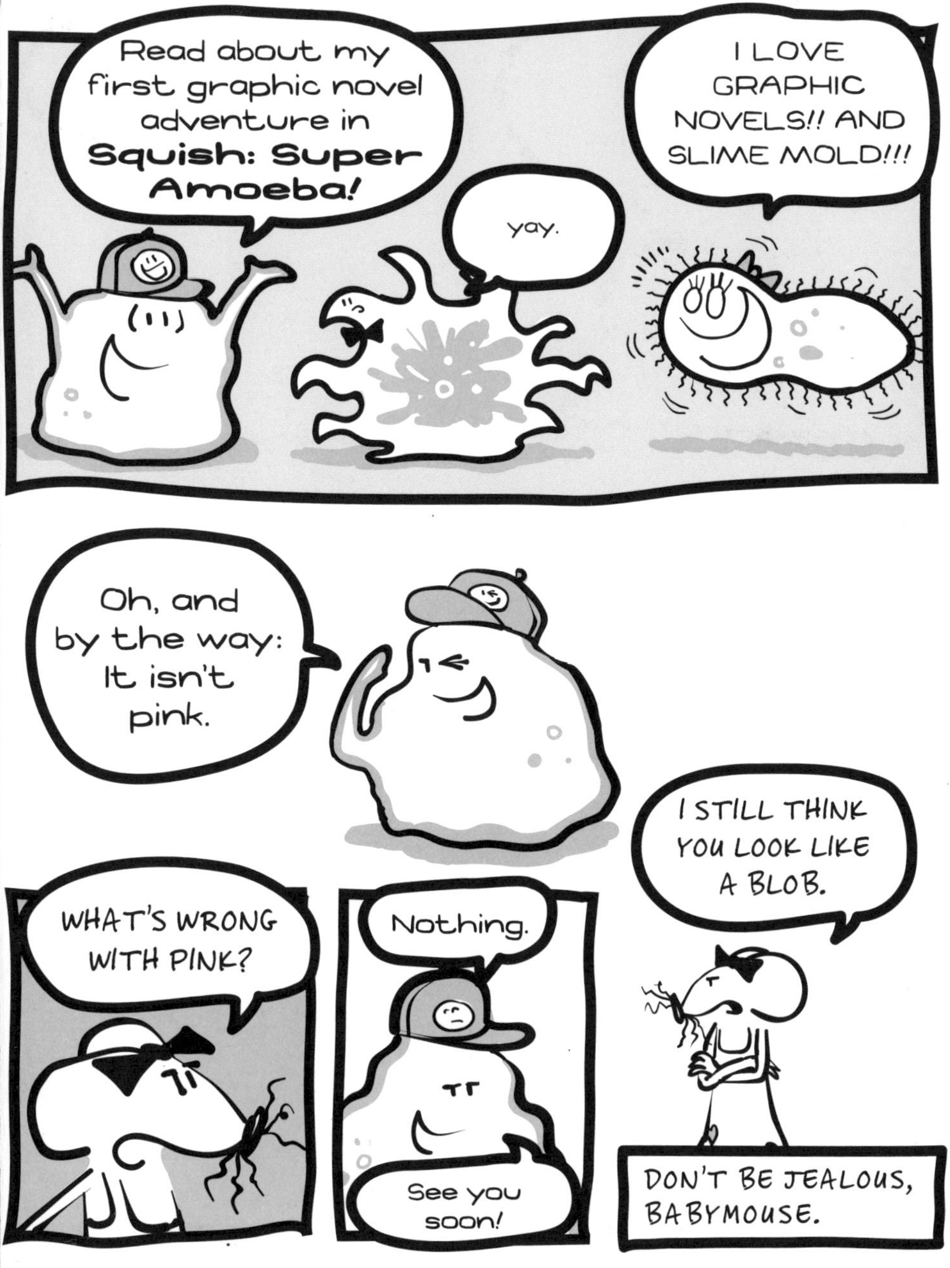
Read about my first graphic novel adventure in **Squish: Super Amoeba!**
yay.
I LOVE GRAPHIC NOVELS!! AND SLIME MOLD!!!
Oh, and by the way: It isn't pink.
WHAT'S WRONG WITH PINK?
Nothing.
See you soon!
I STILL THINK YOU LOOK LIKE A BLOB.
DON'T BE JEALOUS, BABYMOUSE.

If you like Babymouse,
you'll love these other great books
by Jennifer L. Holm!

THE BOSTON JANE TRILOGY
EIGHTH GRADE IS MAKING ME SICK
MIDDLE SCHOOL IS WORSE THAN MEATLOAF
OUR ONLY MAY AMELIA
PENNY FROM HEAVEN
TURTLE IN PARADISE

THEY'RE
REALLY GOOD!
TRUST ME!